The Girl Who Was Born That Way

The Girl Who Was Born That Way

a novella
Gail Benick

inanna poetry & fiction series

**INANNA PUBLICATIONS AND EDUCATION INC.
TORONTO, CANADA**

Copyright © 2015 Gail Benick

Except for the use of short passages for review purposes, no part of this book may be reproduced, in part or in whole, or transmitted in any form or by any means, electronically or mechanically, including photocopying, recording, or any information or storage retrieval system, without prior permission in writing from the publisher.

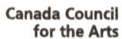  

We gratefully acknowledge the support of the Canada Council for the Arts and the Ontario Arts Council for our publishing program, and the financial assistance of the Government of Canada through the Canada Book Fund.

The Girl Who Was Born That Way is a work of fiction. All the characters and situations portrayed in this book are fictitious and any resemblance to persons living or dead is purely coincidental.

Cover design: Val Fullard

Library and Archives Canada Cataloguing in Publication

Benick, Gail, 1945–, author
    The girl who was born that way / Gail Benick.

(Inanna poetry and fiction series)
Issued in print and electronic formats.
ISBN 978-1-77133-213-2 (pbk.). — ISBN 978-1-77133-214-9 (epub). — ISBN 978-1-77133-216-3 (pdf)

    I. Title. II. Series: Inanna poetry and fiction series

PS8603.E5567G57 2015   C813'.6   C2015-902262-2
                                                                      C2015-902263-0

Printed and bound in Canada

Inanna Publications and Education Inc.
210 Founders College, York University
4700 Keele Street, Toronto, Ontario, Canada M3J 1P3
Telephone: (416) 736-5356 Fax: (416) 736-5765
Email: inanna.publications@inanna.ca   Website: www.inanna.ca

*To the memory of Sherron Sue Benick
With love.*

Parenting is no sport for perfectionists.
—Andrew Solomon, *Far from the Tree*

One

I WANTED TO TAKE MY SISTER'S PICTURE because the mirror in her bedroom was lying to her. Before we went outside, I reread the instructions that came with my Brownie Hawkeye, this time more carefully to take the truest possible snapshot.

#1 Make it interesting. Your picture should tell a story at a glance. Always stand steady, hold your breath and release the shutter with a smooth squeeze action.

I told Terry Sue to stand facing the sun and do something interesting, like wave goodbye at the front door. She was wearing a cardigan sweater and a satin bow anchored with a bobby pin to her thinning hair. The scratches on her scalp — I could hardly see them — came from the sharp metal end of the bobby pin. The rubber tip had fallen off when she opened it with her teeth, a habit Mama hated.

"Don't breathe," I said to Terry Sue. My eye focused on the viewfinder image of her, stiff as a skeleton. Her skin was greyish blue, the bones in her hands jutting out from her flesh. Standing on the porch, skinny and shivering, she looked the opposite of our family's favourite saying: 'Thin is good; thinner is better.' My older sisters, Hetty and Tilya, made up that gem, but even they would agree that our sister who was third in line had gone too far.

"Stop," she said to me on the porch. "Your finger is covering the lens." I moved it, trying to keep the shrunken Terry Sue centered in the frame at least until I punched my finger as hard as I could on the shutter release.

#2 *Double Exposure: Two pictures accidentally taken on one film. It won't happen if you wind the film immediately after taking each picture.*

We sat on the front steps after school, elbows propped on our knees, in the pale light of October. Our eyes searched the street for Papa who had promised to take us to a special event, some sort of a parade, downtown, in St. Louis. I felt excited. And relieved. I would go anywhere to get away from the smell lingering in our kitchen. All houses had their own smells. I knew that from my best friend Fruma Goldfarb's house that always reminded me of herring. But ours stank from something much worse: kasha. Mama made kasha *varnishkes* every Sunday. She never cooked the bowtie pasta until just before she served brisket for dinner. "Your Auntie Tzophia would prepare hers with lots of kasha and not so many bows," Mama repeated each time she made the dish. "My recipe is more like pasta with some buckwheat, mushrooms, and onion tossed in." At the mention of Tzophia, the tears began, like pools of sadness rippling through her to us.

I didn't need to ask who Aunt Tzophia was. One Sunday several months ago, as Mama was roasting the dry kasha in a hot pan, she started to tell us about her younger sister who was called Tzofie for short. Hetty had interrupted. "That frying pan is smoking, Mama." The kasha was already sticking and turning black. "You're going to start a fire in here."

Using a wooden spoon, Mama shuffled the kasha around in the pan. "You remember, Hetty, how we left Lodz with Aunt

Tzophie and Uncle Shmul?" I waited for my sister to answer, but she didn't.

"Hetty," Mama went on. "Remember how we packed the tea cups, forks, knives, and my bubbie's candlesticks into a suitcase? "

I said, "Hetty isn't in the kitchen anymore, Mama."

"All of us together, we went to Warsaw in a buggy pulled by a horse. Late at night."

"Mama, she's not here."

"Do you remember your little cousins Shana and Yitzy went with us?" She had removed the kasha from the heat. "How, when Papa and I decided to came back to Lodz with you, we never saw any of them again?"

I gazed at Terry Sue now, hunched next to me on the porch. When had she stopped eating Mama's kasha? Don't know. As I advanced the film, the clicking of the plastic knob seemed to startle her. Seven exposures were left.

"Don't you dare show that picture of me to anyone." She sat up and wrapped her arms around her chest. "I'm so fat."

#3 Dirty lens. Your camera cannot see through a dirty lens. Keep it clean; it pays. Use Kodak Lens Cleaning Paper and Kodak Lens Cleaner.

Papa made the decision to take Terry Sue and me to the Veiled Prophet parade because of his friend Chaim Rubenstein. The Rubenstein family had come for Sunday dinner the week before the parade. Rebecca Rubenstein, their fourteen-year-old daughter, sat with Terry Sue and me at the kids' end of the table, talking a mile a minute about a big event held annually in St. Louis.

"Jewish girls don't go to the Veiled Prophet Ball," she said. For a reason I couldn't explain — she was either religious or more likely a show off — Rebecca's head was covered by a white beret worn slouchy and tilted to one side. Hatless, Terry Sue and I looked like the poor country cousins, yokels in our own dining room. Rebecca sighed. "Because Jews are not invited."

Moments later, Mama appeared from the kitchen with the kasha varnishkes and brisket, cut in thick chunks, surrounded on the platter by mini potatoes. Fanny Rubenstein, Chaim Rubensteain's wife, said, "Imagine that in 1958! The war may be over but Jews are not allowed in lots of places in this city." I stared at her honey-coloured hair, fixed in a beehive with a can of hair spray. Chaim Rubenstein touched his wife's arm, but she continued: "Jews are never on the guest list to witness the Veiled Prophet crown his Queen of Love and Beauty in the exclusive ballroom of the Chase Park Plaza Hotel."

"Oooo la la," said Rebecca. "And swanky debutantes will be presented to the who's who of St. Louis, too."

"Also not Jewish," her mother said.

Papa suggested that we bless the wine before the meal, though Fanny and Rebecca Rubenstein had wrecked my appetite. I overheard him questioning Chaim Rubenstein about this mysterious man who covered his face with a veil. "What kind of prophet is he?" Papa asked. "Like Moses?"

Chaim Rubenstein lowered his voice. It sounded like he whispered the word God.

Fanny Rubenstein said, "Of course, every child in St. Louis can attend the parade. It's always in autumn around the time of Sukkot." Glancing at the trees almost barren in the twilight, I noticed a lone cardinal perched on a twig. I loved red birds. "And you'll be able to see the Queen of Love and Beauty with her Maids of Honour riding on the floats," Fanny Rubeinstein enthused, "even if you can't go to the VP ball."

Rebecca, spooning a few bowties and kasha onto her plate, gave us a know-it-all smile. Her beret did not budge.

From the moment the Rubensteins mentioned the Queen of Love and Beauty that night and described her Maids of Honour, Terry Sue seemed to enter a society girl fantasy, as if she were a debutante being presented at the VP ball. During dinner, she had pushed up the sleeves of her sweater and pretended to be smoothing gloves — probably like those long white ones worn by Grace Kelly — over her hands and up her arms. Then she dabbed her baby finger into the lukewarm tea and stroked her eyebrows until they resembled half moons. She had eaten next to nothing (that's what Mama said), but when Fanny Rubenstein told Papa that every child in St. Louis could attend the VP parade, Terry Sue sprang from her seat, raced around the table and kissed him on the cheek.

Hetty said, "You mean, the parade is kosher, and the snooty ball isn't?" Papa gave her a stern look, as if to say that his twenty-three year old daughter, his first-born child, should know better. But the Rubensteins paid no attention. The three of them launched into the story of the St. Louis Veiled Prophet parade that seemed longer than the Mississippi and a lot more twisty. "It dates back to 1878," Chaim Rubeinstein told us.

"And once," Fanny Rubenstein added, "a national plowing contest took place on parade day."

"Plowing?" Papa said, jerking his head upright. His attention seemed to be wandering. "*Nu*," he murmured, "it was the harvest time, like Sukkot." When Mama finally sat down next to Papa at the table, he began to sing "My Sukkaleh," a Yiddish song Papa sang every year for the holiday, but this time more slowly, almost in a broken voice, stretching the ending of each word, raising the silver wine goblet between verses and lifting his eyes, as if he expected to find Aunt Tzophie, her husband and two children on the road from Warsaw to Lodz.

"What about the Queen of Love and Beauty?" Terry Sue had asked the minute the Rubensteins left. "They didn't even tell us who she is." Icky bits of brisket and kasha clung to the dirty dishes piled on the kitchen counter. Tea bags floating in lemon-coloured water sat in glass cups stacked four high, one smudged by Fanny Rubenstein's dark lipstick and another by Rebecca's lighter pink shade.

Just then, Tilya returned home. She had missed Sunday dinner with the Rubensteins to research her first philosophy paper at Washington University (about someone important, a German philosopher named Haggle or something like that). She studied the mess: "This kitchen looks like a tornado hit it."

Hetty glared at Tilya who just stood there. Hetty wrapped the leftovers and crammed them into the packed ice box. "Don't get Mama started on tornadoes, all right?"

Everyone in the family knew that any mention of bad weather alarmed Mama who always rocked back and forth, from heel to toe, toe to heel, as soon as the weatherman reported a sighting of a funnel cloud in Missouri, Kansas, Alabama, or Tennessee. She would remind us of the tornado that had touched down in St. Louis in 1950. The winds were so strong that the feathers were plucked right off a chicken. So, I thought, why hadn't the Rubensteins said a word about the threat of tornadoes ever ruining the Veiled Prophet parade? Maybe the prophet had some magic power to make tornadoes go away. Nothing seemed to stop him.

"*Mann tracht*," Mama said into the air. "*Und Gott lacht.*" I didn't understand what that meant or why she was wringing her hands.

"What's Mama so agitated about?" Tilya asked.

"The Veiled Prophet parade." Hetty continued to run water into the burnt roasting pan and placed it on the top of the stove to soak overnight. She told Terry Sue and me to finish clearing the dining room table, which we did not do immediately. Mama was shaking, like a spooked horse I once saw on TV.

"All of a sudden I should love parades?"

"It's just a stupid procession, Mama," Hetty said. "How in the world can you be so afraid of people dressed in costumes parading by you?"

"Like the Nazis marching into Poland. I'll give you parades." Hetty searched for Tilya's eyes, but I noticed that their usual agreement on unspoken things seemed to be missing. I jumped in because any idiot could figure out that the Rubensteins hadn't told us everything.

"I still don't understand why the prophet wears a veil."

"So nobody will know who he is, dummy," Tilya said. Since starting university, she spoke with a new kind of smartness as if she was seeing the world for the first time through a properly cleaned lens. "He wears a white sheet and covers his face with a mask to be really secretive and scary. Just put two plus two together, stupid. The Veiled Prophet belongs to the Ku Klux Klan. I could be wrong, but that's what I heard somewhere. Why else would he wear a pointy hat and carry a shotgun?"

"That's not what the Rubensteins said, Tilya."

Hetty tried to avoid any further talk of the prophet, particularly in front of Mama, by insisting that Terry Sue and I retrieve every dessert dish, wine glass and serving spoon from the dining room. It was too late to ask Tilya to explain more about the Ku Klux Klan. She could, however, have said whether the Veiled Prophet still carried a shotgun. Terry Sue and I threw away all the crumpled dinner napkins and tucked the seats of the dining room chairs under the table before going to bed.

#4 Subject partly cut off: This is merely another case of careless view finding. Keep your eye on the viewfinder image and keep the subject accurately framed until after the shutter clicks.

On the night of the parade, Terry Sue stood close to me, her eyes pressed against the window of the garment factory where father worked on Washington Avenue. From the second floor of his building, we saw thousands of people lining the parade route along the streets of downtown St. Louis. It was still light enough to see Miss Hulling's Cafeteria on the corner of Olive and Eighth where Papa and Chaim Rubenstein sometimes stopped for coffee and fresh fruit pie. Then Papa showed us the big table where he cut dresses from bolts of cotton and offered to make one for Terry Sue in whatever colour she wanted. I tried to imagine her in a sleeveless summer shift, her arms stick-figure thin, like a skeleton swinging from the gallows in a game of Hangman.

"Papa," I said, taking a rough measurement of her wrist with my thumb and middle finger. "Can you make a dress for Terry Sue with long sleeves and cuffs?"

Soon the floats began to pass in front of us. One featured a circus with clowns juggling balls and an elephant squirting water into the crowd. Another was decorated as a saloon in the Wild West with men dressed up like cowboys and cowgirls. My eyes fastened on the piano player in the saloon though I could barely hear the notes he was playing. His left pant leg dangled loosely over the bench with a knot tied at the bottom.

"Where's the piano player's foot?" I asked. My toes started to squirm in my saddle shoes that were laced too tightly.

"He probably lost his leg in the Korean War," Papa said.

I cringed and glanced at Terry Sue, afraid something awful was going to happen to her. She didn't smile or speak, even when I nudged her. She stood at the factory window, waiting.

"Old money," Papa said when eight horses came clopping down the parade route, pulling the float with the Veiled Prophet. "Those, my *kinder*, are the famous Budweiser Clydesdales owned by Augie Busch." He put his arms around us, pulling our bodies closer to his. I was leaning forward, impressed by the height of the Clydesdales with their strong legs, white and feathery, and hooves lifting high off the pavement, when I saw a kid on the street below, standing on the shoulders of two other boys.

"What's in that kid's hand?" I nudged Terry Sue again and pointed to the three boys making a human pyramid, sort of like in gym class. "Can't you see the one standing on top is holding something orange up to his lips, like a straw?" A beer bottle flew through the air, just missing the side of the boy's face, crashing into the Wild West float. Through the factory window, I watched several other kids barrel into the pyramid and knock over the boy with the straw. Shots were fired from somewhere as the crowd began to disperse along Washington Avenue. I was looking through the viewfinder of my Brownie Hawkeye, trying as best I could to frame exactly what I was seeing on the street, but before I could snap the picture, Papa moved us away from the window.

"You've had enough," he said. "There's too much commotion going on down there." Terry Sue begged to stay for the rest of the parade, pleaded to see the fairy Queen of Love and Beauty, but Papa, in a quiet voice, said that it was getting late and we should leave. Terry Sue, without dropping her eyes from his face, said all right.

The bus ride went fast, with Papa squeezed between Terry Sue and me on the seat behind the rear door. Not sleepy, we pestered him for a story about something.

Terry Sue wanted to hear more about the Queen of Love and Beauty. "Who was she?" she asked Papa. "Does she live in a castle? How was she chosen?" He shook his head, clueless as we were.

"Okay," I said. "Then maybe you can tell us what really happened in the end to Aunt Tzophie, her husband and their two children in Poland."

Papa hesitated, becoming sad, well, very sad.

"Did they find a place to live in Warsaw?" I persisted. "Where did our cousins go to school? Does Aunt Tzophie still make kasha varnishkes with more kasha and not so many bowties?"

No answer.

On Delmar and Purdue, we got off the bus. The streets were empty as the three of us walked home.

#5 Subject out of focus: This kind of fuzzy-wuzzy comes up when you take pictures closer than five feet. Close-ups can be made with a Kodak Close-Up Attachment No. 13.

The morning after we went to the Veiled Prophet parade, the *Post Dispatch* was spread across the table at breakfast. Mama was still in bed when Papa put on his glasses and read aloud a short report he found in the bottom corner of the front page:

> St. Louis. Police arrested a suspect in a pea-shooting incident at the Veiled Prophet parade last night that left one Clydesdale with a bloody eye, a float damaged and the Veiled Prophet unharmed. The suspect, a thirteen-year-old Negro male residing in the Pruitt-Igoe Public Housing Project, was taken into custody and is being held on charges of juvenile delinquency. In an unrelated incident, police found a Red Ryder BB gun on the roof of a garment factory located on Washington and Eighth while they were investigating shots fired into the crowd. No further arrests were made.

Without a care for the arrested pea-shooter or the bleeding Clydesdale, I turned to Papa. Between gulps of orange juice, I cried that we had left the parade too early for me to take any good photos of the Veiled Prophet or the Queen of Love and Beauty.

Tilya said, "It was probably too dark anyway so stop *kvetching* about it." I looked at her wet hair smelling of Breck shampoo, jealous of how the glossy strands hung straight to her collarbones. She grabbed the last bagel to eat during her philosophy lecture. "Don't you know anything about cameras, Linda Sue?" Tilya said to me over her shoulder. "That Brownie Hawkeye of yours isn't even the Flash model."

The door slammed as I was about to explain. I wanted to tell Tilya that the Hawkeye Flash model was not what I needed. I had to have the Close Up Attachment #13 to take a true picture of Terry Sue without any fuzzy-wuzzies, to show her how she really looked, before it was too late.

October 13, 1961

Dearest baby sister (she wrote to me from Renard Hospital, Children's Psychiatry),

I've only been here a couple of weeks, but trust me, Linda Sue, I'm trying to do everything they tell me so I can come home soon. I promise. There are lots of little rules here, like finishing the whole muffin you're given for snack and not stuffing part of it into your socks. But there are some fun activities, too. Dr. Ryan has been very good in letting me do things. I've been to the American Theatre to see a play about Helen Keller, gone swimming at the Missouri School for the Blind, and I hope to go bowling on the weekend.

Right this minute I'm looking at the autumn colours through my hospital window. Don't the reds and golds always remind you of Sukkot? Remember how we made long paper chains to decorate the Sukkah at Sunday school and hung plastic apples and oranges from the ceiling? Fall is truly my favourite season.

We used to have so much fun trick-or-treating on Halloween.

I still want to vomit whenever I remember the time the Rubensteins came to our house one year in October. It seems like a million years ago. Maybe it was 1958. Why did Papa invite them anyway? Ever since Rebecca Rubenstein mentioned the Veiled Prophet Ball at dinner, all I could think about was being skinny enough to be a debutante. Even a little skinnier than I already was. Did I tell you that I found a picture of the VP Queen of Love and Beauty in Life Magazine? *She was so thin and beautiful in a white brocade dress and a tiara with a plume on top. I was heartbroken when we didn't get to see the queen's float the only year we went to the parade with Papa. I still don't think it was so dangerous to be at the parade. I'm sure those gun shots we heard were from a toy gun. I was 12 years old then, but you were only 10, much too young to get what was happening. Anyway, wouldn't you love to be the VP queen? I'd give anything to be her, even for a day.*

Love ya always, Terry Sue

P.S. Dr. Ryan says I will be moved down to a lower floor soon if everything continues to go well so I hope it won't be long until I see you again.

Love again, T.S.

Two

"**A**ND DON'T FORGET THE RECEIPT," she yelled to Hetty from upstairs in her bedroom. "The salesgirl in that department store doesn't know you from Adam." Mama separated *department* into three distinct syllables. Four if you count the "a" she always inserted after "depart."

I expected Hetty to respond, say something, but instead she took the Famous Barr shopping bag off the dining room table and hurried me out the front door.

"Hey, what's the big rush?" I didn't understand why she was so keen to exchange the circular skirt with a poodle on it she bought last Saturday for a pleated skirt. Were poodle skirts out of style already? I wondered. Hetty would know. She was the oldest sister, the family fashion plate, the one who woke up and announced, before a tooth had been brushed or a zit squeezed, that all four of us MUST wear the most popular, beautiful thing. I skipped down the street, trailing a couple of feet behind her, humming a rhyme Tilya repeated often: "You must, you must, you must develop your bust." I could see my breath in the cold November air.

Hetty waited for me at the intersection of Amherst and Vanderbilt before crossing to Jackson Park. I took her hand though I didn't really need to and scrunched up my eyebrows at her to show that I was old enough to cross by myself.

I had always wondered why Mama and Papa named her Hetty. It seemed out of place in our ivy-covered neighbourhood where streets were named after universities — Cornell, Dartmouth or Stanford — and lots of girls at school were called Linda, Diane or Carol. We lived on Tulane, which was also a university somewhere, but not, my sisters said, in the state of Missouri. I had to admit that University City was the best place in the world to grow up. Whenever I rode my bike down the hill into the park and stopped to watch the heartthrob, Myron K., playing a game of three-on-three, I felt sorry for Hetty and Tilya who had spent their childhoods in Lodz, probably cooped up in small rooms. They never spoke about any parks there.

"Hetty," I said as we entered Jackson Park. "I always forget why Mama and Papa named you Hetty."

She glanced at me sideways. "I told you a thousand times. It's short for Henrietta."

"Who's she again?" I could see

"Don't worry. Not your *bubbie*."

"Maybe it's short for Heinrich." I knew that even the hint of a boy's name would upset her. Girls, I read in her *Seventeen Magazine*, had to be one hundred percent girls with frilly clothes and names that sounded like they belonged just to girls. "And," I said to her. "If you were an English person, you might be called Henry or Harry, but only if you were a boy."

"Henrietta is for Henrietta Szold." The dead sound of her voice meant either that I was bothering her or she wasn't in a good mood. The Famous Barr bag hanging from her wrist crinkled as we walked. "You know, Henrietta Szold was the founder of Haddasah."

"Why would you be named after her?"

"How should I know?" Hetty didn't want to answer me. She and I both knew that Mama loved Henrietta Szold. She would tell us to be *menschlich* like Henrietta Szold whenever she wanted us to be kind and caring. It was always Henrietta Szold founded this hospital and established that medical school in Israel.

"Maybe she thought you'd become a Zionist pioneer," I said although it was hard to imagine my fashionable sister living on a kibbutz and sloshing around in rubber boots. "Hetty, what's a Zionist again?"

She took my hand as we approached Delmar. "Nothing like me."

"You don't want to go to Israel?"

"I'm here now," Hetty said. "And that's nothing to sneeze at." She tugged me across the street, both of us practically running, to meet Joyce Hirschfield, her best friend who was joining us on our hunt for Hetty's new pleated skirt.

"Anyway, if Mama loves Henrietta Szold so much," I said, "Why didn't she just name you Hadassah?" I dropped her hand and darted ahead of her.

"You want me to show up in U. City with a name like that? It's embarrassing enough that our sister looks like a walking stick. Maybe I should wear a *babushka* on my head and speak Yiddish on the bus, too."

"Okay, but Hadassah is a nice name, don't you think?"

"Yeah, for somewhere else."

Joyce Hirschfield was slouched over the cosmetics counter at the department store's entrance when we arrived. She reeked of the perfume she had been sampling, likely spraying her ear lobes with all sorts of fragrances.

"What's that vile smell you're wearing?" Hetty asked. Glass bottles in the shape of triangles and hearts dotted the counter, some decorated with swirling lines and topped with plump stoppers.

Joyce said, "Where were you?" For as far back as I could remember, Hetty's friend Joyce had a temper that could flare up as quickly as a runaway pony. I was afraid of her when she came to our house, terrified that one of us would say something to make her explode.

"First tell me, what kind of perfume are you wearing?" Hetty asked.

"Hetty, you're twenty minutes late." Joyce tapped her foot on the floor of Famous Barr. She seemed to have a lot of nervous tics, like toe tapping, when she was angry.

Hetty said, "Is it skunk or something?"

"White Shoulders, you idiot. And it's eau de cologne." Joyce said. She sniffed the inside of her wrist and passed it in front of my nose.

I felt too dizzy to concentrate on what they were saying. "Oh, barf," I mumbled. The musky odour made me gag, like walking into a public restroom.

I think Joyce was trying to make Hetty and me feel bad because we were late. I didn't catch the beginning of what Joyce said to Hetty, but it sounded something like, you better watch out.

Then Joyce raised her voice and said in a threatening way: "God is going to punish both of you for shopping on Shabbat."

I thought, how would Joyce know what God might do to us? Wasn't that why we went to Sunday school — to learn about God and how to follow His commandments? Actually, I went to pray for Terry Sue.

"Fat chance," Hetty said. She didn't question whether Joyce should speak for God or not. Beads of perspiration gathered on Hetty's forehead.

"It's a pretty long *schlep* from U. City to here," she said, giving Joyce an unmistakable kick in the shoe. "And you sound just like my mother who is driving me crazy."

"All right already," Joyce said. I gazed at the huge width of Famous Barr. Its walls were curved, like nothing I'd seen in other department stores. I guess that was to be expected in

Clayton that was more on the rich side than University City.

Hetty said: "Easy for you to say."

Joyce picked up the pink box of White Shoulders and fingered it, caressing the gold cameo embossed on the front. "So whose mom is perfect?" she said.

"You don't understand. My mother hardly gets out of bed anymore." Hetty's bottom lip quaked a tiny bit when she said this. I felt sorry for her. The truth is, I felt sad for all of us.

"You're kidding, right?" Joyce said.

"Complains constantly of headaches."

I sprinkled some cologne on my neck to hide the sour smell of sweat. "Is that why there are so many Aspirin bottles turned upside down on her night table?" I asked. They glanced at each other over my head, surprised I was paying attention.

"All day she's in bed? That's unreal," Joyce said.

"Stop with the questions." Hetty looked away. "It sounds like you're from Children's Aid or something." An elderly gentleman passed by the perfume counter and tipped his wide-brimmed hat at us. Hetty clutched my elbow. I'm not sure why because Famous Barr felt completely safe. Everyone knew that the owners, the May family, were Jewish.

"Hetty, is May the real name of the people who own this store?" I asked. "Or was it shortened, like ours?" We went from Berkowitz to Berk, my father once told us, with the flick of an immigration officer's pen.

Joyce said, "I've always liked your mother."

"A person can change." I noticed Hetty wasn't looking at her. When she gripped the counter top, I saw her fingernails. They were bitten so badly that I wondered if they hurt. "Trust me," she said.

"You mean more American?" said Joyce.

"No, I mean more in her room."

"Since when?"

"Since she found out something's screwed up with Terry Sue," Hetty said.

My head sunk down almost as low as my shoulder blades. I wished Hetty wouldn't talk to Joyce Hirschfield or any of her other friends about us.

"What about Terry Sue?" Joyce said.

Hetty tightened the muscles in her jaw. "I'm not sure."

Joyce put down the box of White Shoulders. "Well, you must be wilfully blind or something not to notice that there's a problem." She started to walk from perfumes to men's socks. I didn't know if she was looking for a six-pack of athletic socks for her two brothers, or dressy black socks for her father. At least she had brothers. Myself, I'm happy with a family of four sisters. But our parents, I have a feeling, would have liked one of us to be a boy. I watched as Joyce slipped a pair of charcoal-gray argyles into Hetty's shopping bag without paying for them.

"My mother wants me to postpone the wedding," Hetty said.

"Because of your sister?"

"You know, Joyce, you're not listening to a word I say."

We took the escalator up to women's clothing on the second floor. If Joyce Hirschfield suspected something about Terry Sue, it suddenly hit me, everyone in University City might know this secret something. That included Hetty's boyfriend Lenny Abrams who could decide not to marry her. Our parents would *plotz* if that happened. They'd already booked Beth Israel for the wedding months ago.

"I want to make an exchange, please." Hetty said as she returned her poodle skirt to the salesperson.

"Do you have the receipt?" The saleslady's hair was tucked into a no-monkey-business bun. She seemed eager to catch my sister in a mistake that only an amateur shopper — a person who did not observe the rules of shopping in the respectful way that Hetty did — would make. "We don't make exchanges without it, Miss."

Hetty reached into the Famous Barr bag and freed the folded bill from the tissue paper rustling inside. It passed between them without a word spoken.

The prospect of Hetty's wedding rattled our family, as if a foreign object was about to invade our private world. Because there was something strictly between us, a feeling so inward and completely our own, that we had no intention of showing it to anyone else.

Hetty tried to cover it with clothes. She obsessed about what we would wear to Beth Israel, not for the wedding, but for the *aufruf* ceremony when she and Lenny would be called up to the Torah for a blessing. For the first time, the Berks, all six of us, would be on view at the ritzy shul of Lenny's parents. The *aufruf* was scheduled for the last Shabbat morning in January, and every Saturday leading up to that day, Hetty and Joyce combed the expensive department stores looking for the right outfit for Mama, for me, and, most of all, for Terry Sue. One week they shopped at Scruggs Vandervoot and Barney and the next time, they went to Stix, Baer and Fuller. Receipts were kept and exchanges frequently made.

"Does this blouse hide Terry Sue's arms enough?" Hetty asked us one night after dinner. She had organized a family fashion show in the living room. "And what about her chest?"

"What about it?" I said. Whenever I bathed with Terry Sue, I couldn't help noticing that her chest was much wider than mine, like a broad, flat plate of armour with two pale dots for nipples at the far edges.

"The colour of that blouse — it's called chartreuse or something — makes me want to puke," Tilya said, eying the matching skirt. "I'd call it vomitious green." She looked at Terry Sue more closely. "And why can't you stand up straight and stick your boobs out a little?" Wearing a fitted sweater, Tilya thrust her uplifted chest in the direction of Terry Sue. "Like that Queen of Love and Beauty you idolize or Marilyn Monroe."

"Maybe Terry Sue should wear falsies under her blouse," I said, "to make her bosom look bigger."

"*Got* forbid," mother said. Curled on the sofa wearing a rumpled housedress, she seemed more absent than present. She hardly managed to sweep the kitchen floor most days. Still, she was interested in the tiniest details of the wedding: the texture of the tablecloths, the pattern on the cutlery, the printing on the place cards, the price of the matchbook favours. It didn't seem to matter if the marriage occurred today, tomorrow or not at all.

Dusk made the aqua walls of the living room a deeper shade of blue. Rays of darkness fell on mother's face, as if the something terrible were etched on the lenses of her eyes. "*Got* forbid," she said again. Sinking further into the folds of the slip-covered sofa, she sounded far away. Her voice cracked as if a child was being torn from her.

Tilya walked over to the windows and closed the metal slats of the Venetian blinds to shut out a draft of cold air coming from outside. She turned to us, her pointy boobs hiked up almost to her neck.

"When I graduate from Wash U.," she said, "I'm changing my name to Toni."

We were quiet for a few seconds and then I got up to go to my room. I opened the bottom drawer of my dresser where I kept a cigar box with my allowance in it. I was saving up for the Brownie Close Up Attachment #13 so that I could take crystal clear pictures of Terry Sue when she wasn't so stiff and posed, to capture her secret smiles, half grins — all the things you'd want the world to know about someone you loved who might be dying. I counted the money in the cigar box. There probably wasn't enough to buy Terry Sue a padded brassier at Famous Barr. But I could go to Woolworths and buy some foam rubber to make falsies for her. Which I did two days later.

November 19, 1961

Dear best-dressed big sister in the whole wide world (she wrote to Hetty from Renard Hospital, Children's Psychiatry),
I want to tell you something horrible, Hetty. It's like a confession that I need to make and I can only tell you because you are, after all, the oldest of the four of us. I feel I owe you and everyone in our family an explanation. Do you remember your aufruf *at Beth Israel on that freezing day in January? I can't believe I still remember anything from 1959, but I just can't forget what happened there. You know, I was never in a modern synagogue like Beth Israel before. So many seats had gold name plates on them, and I wasn't sure if we were allowed to sit in someone else's seat. So I just sat down next to Mama. Papa was on her other side. She kept looking up at the big curved ceiling and moaning, "God forbid, god forbid," like she was begging God to keep something unwanted from happening. Light poured in from a row of windows way, way up high. Do you remember that? So many people were there for Shabbat services that morning, all horsed up in their herringbone tweeds and silk scarves. You and Lenny looked really good. That bright blue dress did a lot for your hair. When you went up to the bimah to recite the blessing, I thought I would die. I was just so happy for you, really I was overjoyed. Did I ever tell you that someone in front of me said to the woman next to her that it was strange to have an* aufruf *so many months before the wedding? Is that true?*

I'm not sure you knew that Mama was crying the whole time. She was trying to hold it in, but tears were rolling down her face and she kept wiping them away with a dirty Kleenex and muttering under her breath, "God forbid." You know she forced me to carry those stupid candies into the sanctuary covered in a basket. I felt so idiotic walking around carrying a silly basket filled with soft candies, like I was a five-year-old or something, As soon as the blessing was over, Mama poked me and said to run up to you and Lenny on the bimah and pour the candies on your heads. I didn't want to do it, but she gave me one of her looks. Lenny had to bend over really far so that I could reach the top of his head. His kippah nearly slid off his head. Suddenly everyone was laughing at me. I know they were all wondering who was that little girl because I'm so short. But I wasn't a baby at all. Really, I swear, I didn't want to carry the candy. I swear it wasn't my idea to throw it on your heads. Mama made me do it. She said it meant that you and Lenny would have a sweet start to your married life. I hope you will forgive me for embarrassing the family. But at least Mama didn't throw one of her conniption fits and really humiliate us in front of the whole world.

By the way, did you like that yellowy-green skirt and blouse I was wearing that day? They're much too big on me now because I lost a few more pounds recently. I swim around in them like a fish in deep water. You can borrow the outfit if there's ever another *aufruf in the family*. But it won't be my *aufruf because nobody will ever want to marry me*. Don't ask me how I know. I just know that I'm the only person in the world like me. Who would ever marry a one of a kind?

Love ya tons and tons, Terry Sue

P.S. Dr. Ryan says that if I lose more than 3 other pounds, he's going to put me on a feeding tube. Over my dead body.

Could you look for those falsies Linda Sue once made for me. They may come in handy. I hope I will be with you next Thanksgiving.

   Love again, T.S.

Three

ON THE FIRST NIGHT OF HANUKAH, while Hetty shredded potatoes and grated onions, Tilya was busy coring apples. She tinkered with the recipe for applesauce, omitting, without telling us, the half cup of sugar recommended by Irma Rombaur in *The Joy of Cooking*. Sweet things did not agree with Tilya. But she and Hetty adored *The Joy*. Hetty said the name Rombaur with so much admiration that I mixed up Rombaur with the Rambam, a.k.a. Moses Maimonides, the Torah scholar our rabbi practically worshipped and talked about almost every Sunday.

Terry Sue was standing at the sink. She dug a paring knife into the holes of her *hanukiah*, trying to remove last year's melted wax from the candle holders. Scraps, mostly blue and red, littered the basin.

"Not like that, moron," Tilya said. "You're going to slice off your finger." With a damp sponge, Terry Sue wiped the edges of the holders, which were wedged into the heads of nine ceramic figures of children clasping hands. None of us had ever seen such a cute *hanukiah* before Aunt Mimi gave it to Terry Sue for her tenth birthday. Mine was made of dull brass. Hetty and Tilya shared an oil burning one. (Fruma said oil burning candle holders didn't exist anymore and they might be illegal.)

"Now you're clean and ready," Terry Sue said to the tiny people on her *hanukiah*. Barely four feet tall, with wispy strawberry blond hair parted down the middle, Terry Sue looked like a small child, too.

Tilya took the sliced apples to the stove where she emptied them into a pot brimming with water. She stirred them once and tossed the oversized metal spoon into the sink. When it hit Terry Sue's *hanukiah*, the nose of one little figurine chipped.

"We can still light the candles on your *hanukiah* tonight." I said to Terry Sue as she fled the kitchen, crying. "Father can glue the nose back on when he gets home," I called out after her as she took off. Tilya, as expected, did nothing to stop her or apologize. Tough as a Jewish nail. That's how our family often described her. I didn't understand how a nail could be Jewish, but it was true that Tilya seemed pretty hard a lot of the time. On the back burner of the stove, an icy ball of chicken soup, slowly thawing, began to gurgle. I went over to the sink and picked up Terry Sue's *hanukiah* and the nose from the chipped figurine. I held both in my hands like the parts of a wounded red bird, trembling with tenderness and anger.

Hetty and Tilya continued to prepare the Hanukah dinner by themselves while Mama and Terry Sue stayed upstairs. Papa had not returned from work yet. My two oldest sisters looked like cooks in a restaurant with their hair pulled up in ponytails springing from the back of their heads. Terry Sue and I could never wear high, bouncy ponytails, I thought. My curls were too tight and her hairline was too low on her neck. As Hetty bent forward to plop some of the latke concoction into the frying pan, I noticed, not for the first time, Hetty's long and slender neck. Papa always said his daughters had necks like swans, which didn't include Terry Sue. Something wasn't right about her neck.

I remembered a time, years before, when our family had spent a Labour Day weekend at Aunt Mimi and Uncle Herman's clubhouse in the Ozarks. Really it was more of a dilapidated shack near the Meramec River than a proper cottage. The strong undertow of the Meramec scared me. Every summer someone died on that river, my aunt and uncle said. The shoreline was too rocky to walk along, and it was strewn with cigarette butts and broken beer bottles. So we played in the scrubby fields around the clubhouse instead, wearing halter tops or no tops at all when it was really hot. But Terry Sue preferred to be covered up. Almost always, she put on one of my T-shirts that came to her knees and hung a towel around her neck. Just before we left the Ozarks to come home, the two of us were swinging from a tree branch outside the clubhouse door. (Aunt Mimi said you could tell it was a Sycamore by its greyish white bark and large leaves.) Out of nowhere, Tilya jumped up and yanked Terry Sue's bath towel off her neck, really upsetting Terry Sue.

"You always do that," I said. The palms of my hands felt raw from gripping the Sycamore branch. I didn't know why Tilya would want to embarrass Terry Sue like that. Bored or plain tired of us, probably.

She shrugged. "Do what?"

"You always do mean things to her, Tilya." She looked away from me so I knew my voice must have sounded annoyed. I was annoyed. Most of the other times when Tilya did nasty things to Terry Sue or me, I could see the fun in it.

Then Mama came to the door and said, "What's going on?" as if anyone needed to draw her a picture.

"Well, she's my younger sister," Tilya said. "And I'll do whatever I please."

"It's not fair." When I looked over at Terry Sue, I saw her fleshy neck, so thick and stubby that it looked like she didn't have a neck. Behind her ear, a long fold of skin extended from head to shoulder. "How would you feel if someone treated you like that?" I said.

"Life's not fair," Tilya said. She was getting a little ruffled. "You might as well learn that right now." Still not looking at me.

"I want my towel back," Terry Sue cried out. "I hate my neck." We held onto the branch though the bouncy swing in our legs was gone. When I glanced at Terry Sue, her face seemed to me full of fear and shame, both at once. Tears welled up in her eyes.

"Just think of it like this," Tilya said. "Nobody's going to force you to wear a gold star because of your fat neck."

"What's that supposed to mean?" I let go of the branch and landed solidly on my feet. "Now you've made her cry. You're the meanest person I ever met."

Mama came over to the tree when she heard Terry Sue fall to the ground and helped her brush off dirt from the T-shirt she was wearing. Mama must have understood something about the fold on her neck that she wasn't telling us. Why else did she say that Terry Sue would need surgery very soon to fix it? That was when it dawned on me. Something much worse than neck fat was wrong with Terry Sue, but I didn't know what it was. Mama wouldn't say so I figured it must be something really terrible, something unspeakable.

It took Papa longer than usually to get home from work on that first night of Hanukah because even an inch of snow in St. Louis brought traffic almost to a stop. When he finally arrived, there were only four of us at the dinner table. For some reason, Mama and Terry Sue hadn't come downstairs. We kindled the lights on our *hanukiahs* and said the blessings, but skipped the "little *dreidel*" song. Terry Sue was the only one who still liked to sing it. Papa tried his best to make us happy. He reached into his pants pocket and, as if by a complete miracle, found a silver dollar for each of us. He kissed our foreheads as he pressed the coins into our hands. I saw the corners of his mouth pulling downward that I think meant he was unhappy on the inside.

I stared at Hetty and Tilya's swan-like necks shimmering in the first light of Hanukah, long, smooth and strikingly graceful. Their ponytails bobbed from side to side. Once or twice, I touched the back of my own neck, pinching the skin with my fingertips as hard as I could to create a fold like Terry Sue's. The twisted candles on her cute *hanukiah* were the first to flicker and burn out though she wasn't there to see them melting into nothing or notice that the nose on one of the figurines was still broken. Hetty scraped the latkes from our plates. But the latkes didn't taste like latkes. I think someone forgot to add the flour. Tilya ladled the scalding soup into our bowls, the hand-painted soup bowls mother brought from Lodz, the ones I loved because we only used them when we were together for special occasions and Hanukah was still a special occasion in our family back then.

December 12, 1961

My dear very smart sister (she wrote to Tilya from Renard Hospital, Children's Psychiatry),

I just want to thank you and everyone in our family — you'll thank Mama, Papa, Hetty and Linda Sue, for me, pretty please — for visiting me on Hanukah this year. I know Mama was upset that I wouldn't eat any of the latkes. The greasy smell made me feel sick. But I do love the package of coloured paper and pencils you brought me. I'd like to cut the sheets into little squares like mosaic tiles and paste them into the shape of a flower, but they won't give me permission to have anything sharp. I feel like I'm being watched all the time. Do the nurses think I'm retarded or what? Everyone here is so excited about Christmas. I think I'm the only Jewish girl in this unit. We have a beautiful tree that I helped jazz up with lots of tinsel and strings of popcorn. But it's lonely in the hospital and kind of boring. I've gone through roommates like we used to go through bubble gum. They come and go, but I'm stuck here.

I met with someone named Dr. Richardson yesterday because Mama and Papa are worried that I am not "maturing" as I should, whatever that means. (It might mean my chest is still as flat as a pancake. Sickening, isn't it?) And I'm not growing taller either. I hope I'm not going to be short the rest of my life. It's so embarrassing. Do you remember that time you took me to Heman Park? It was on a Saturday afternoon. A guy drove up to us at the curb in one of those flashy cars. A Buick or an Oldsmobile. "Hey, Little Miss Midget," he said. Don't you remember that time? He smelled like Budweiser and had a cupid tattoo on his arm sticking out the window. "Want a ride, shorty? C'mon. Get in." It was really scary because a man living three doors down from us on Tulane had just been arrested for hiding about a thousand nasty photos of children in his basement. Do you remember him? He was someone's dad. I was thinking what if this guy in the Buick or Oldsmobile was a dad and a pervert, too. Luckily, you dragged me away, like a smart big sister.

By the way, Tilya, a lot of doctors and interns have started to visit me at strange times of the day and smile at me like I'm a funny-looking kid. (Some of the interns are pretty cute!) But none of them will tell me if something is wrong. That's the worst part. I really miss you and the whole family. I feel terrible for making the family come to the hospital to see me. Every night I ask God to keep all of you safe. I feel better knowing God is watching over you. Before I go to sleep, I always say the shema for everyone, even you.

Love ya tons, Terry Sue

P.S. Tilya, I know you probably don't believe in God anymore after studying all those big philosophers at Wash U. But whatever you do, don't tell Mama and Papa. I know Mama would cry and cry about what happened to her second daughter, the genius.

Love again, T.S.

Four

THE WEEKEND BEFORE Terry Sue turned thirteen in 1959, Papa surprised us by proposing a Sunday outing to celebrate. Our family never did any really interesting things. We would never have thought up the idea of going on a picnic hours away from University City. We would have stayed home as usual and gone for a walk. But, a few days before Terry Sue's birthday, Chaim Rubenstein told Papa about a special place to go in the Ozarks.

"Bring your bathing suits, girls," he said on Saturday during lunch. "Chaim Rubenstein — you remember his daughter Rebecca? She came to our house last Sukkot — tells me it's a park with water."

Mama said, "A park? We should drive on highways to get to a park?" Cars terrified her. Actually, she hesitated to leave the house for almost any reason. And the mention of a road trip to an unfamiliar spot caused her to breathe extra quickly. Maybe she feared the wide open spaces or America itself. I wasn't sure.

"Why go? There's a nice park around the corner," she said, unsteady as she tried to carry a tray of cucumbers and tomatoes in one hand and cream cheese in the other. "A *mechaye*.

Papa refused to give in. He was generally more positive than Mama maybe because he read *The Power of Positive Thinking* all the time in bed. Also, he tried to avoid talking about the past. If I asked him why he and Mama didn't have numbers stamped on their arms like their friends who played cards at our house, he changed the subject.

"This Sunday," he said to Mama, "let's go to the Ozarks and try Chaim Rubenstein's idea." He cupped a bagel in his hand and cut it in half with a bread knife, the jagged blade nearly slitting his palm. "Another time we'll stay here and walk to Heman Park."

"I don't want to go to Heman Park for my birthday," Terry Sue said. "It smells like rotten garbage in there from the River des Peres."

"But the River des Peres is only a little creek, silly," Tilya said.

"You know, *mein kinder*," Mama said. Her face was creased with worry lines. "You can drown in a thimble of water." Hetty took the plate of honey cake from the counter and offered a piece to her.

"*Feh*," Mama said, pushing the cake away with her hand. Her baby finger caught the handle of a glass mug filled with hot water. It spilled onto my lap and dripped from one knee down my leg and into my sock. I felt the burn on my ankle the most. I sat there. I knew that if I said one little ouch, Mama would become alarmed. She'd insist that every package of frozen peas and lima beans in the freezer had to be packed onto my ankle instantly. She'd rush to the ice box for butter to put a salve on it. She'd inspect the pinkish spot every three minutes and decide that it was a third degree burn that had to be treated at the Jewish Hospital. Her hysterics would overtake Papa's plans to celebrate Terry Sue's birthday away from home. So I sat there and shut up.

That evening Papa hunched over a worn map of rural Missouri borrowed from Chaim Rubenstein, most likely the first state highway map to be studied as if it were a Talmudic text. He rested his knuckles on place names that we had never dreamed of, let alone spoken in our house: Festus, De Soto, Cape Girardeau.

"It's east of Farmington," he said. "Off Highway 67."

"Farming what?" Mama said. She walked over to the kitchen table, peering over his shoulder. Her hips and shoulders were much wider than his thin slouching frame. She dried her hands on the dishtowel, squeezing it fitfully between her fingers.

He squinted at a dot on the map. "Not farming," he said. "Here's the place Chaim Rubenstein mentioned. It's Johnson something."

"I don't care what Rubenstein told you about Johnson. I'm not going."

"Don't start," Papa said to her. He twisted around and gave her one of those not-in-front-of-the-children looks. I tried to picture Papa steering our used Plymouth on bumpy country roads and Mama sitting on a picnic blanket with the tops of her knee-high hosiery showing. Sometimes it was hard to imagine them existing anywhere outside our kitchen.

Mama did her best to delay our departure on Sunday morning. First, she announced that she had to go to the bathroom. Then she returned to the house because she forgot her pills. She stood for minutes on the front porch landing, reaching out her hand, touching the *mezuzah* attached to the outer doorframe of the house and kissing her fingers. Just touching the *mezuzah*, which contained a prayer from the Torah, seemed to comfort her. At the last moment, she insisted on repacking the trunk in order to separate the jug of grape Kool-Aid from the chopped egg sandwiches. Sitting next to Papa, she whimpered until we left U. City behind.

Terry Sue and I were squished between Hetty and Tilya in the back seat, but we soon flipped around to look out the rear window. In the car right behind us, a girl dangled her small bare feet out the front window.

"Stop leaning on me," Hetty said.

"I'm not touching you," I said. The wind whipped through the half open windows, softening Mama's warning cries: "Slow down! "Brake!" Cars honked as Papa changed lanes without signaling. Once he swerved to avoid a dead opossum. Mama grabbed the wheel before we almost flew off the highway.

"Mama, we're going to have an accident if you keep that up," Hetty shouted from behind.

Tilya tried to distract us. "I spy with my little eye," she said. "Something that starts with the letter B."

"Is it that blue car?" Terry Sue said.

"Nope."

"Is it that billboard?" I asked. Huge advertisements for horse breeders, steak restaurants, and reptile farms peppered the roadside.

"Not exactly," Tilya said.

"What does that mean? It either is or isn't," I said.

"Well, it's an ad, but not on a billboard." I hated the way she always tried to trick us, to make us look stupid, just like her new boyfriend Robby Sloan did. Whenever he came to our house, he walked around spouting quotes from some old Greek play. "Loathing is endless," he would say, puffing a smoke ring into the air. "Hate is a bottomless cup, I pour and pour." A real oddball, father called him. I decided to tell our parents that I saw them both smoking behind the house just last week.

"Then where is the ad?" I asked her.

"Didn't you see the barn about ten minutes ago, advertising the Meramec Caverns? It said the caves were the secret hideout of Jesse James."

"Ten minutes ago. That's not fair." I was mad enough to tell Mama and Papa what else Tilya and Robby were doing behind the house.

"Who cares about Jesse James?" Hetty said.

"I'm thirsty," Terry Sue said. "Can't we stop already?"

Tilya leaned over to tap father on the shoulder. "Let's stop at Dairy Queen for ice cream," she said.

"I want strawberry," said Terry Sue.

"And go shopping." Hetty added. "There are lots of souvenir shops around here."

While our parents waited in line at DQ, the four of us ran next door to Maeve's Curio Shoppe which sold triangular Missouri banners with the slogan "Show Me State" in felt letters, silver-plated spoons, Indian feathers, fake snakes and ash trays made of hammered copper. Cartons of cigarettes were stacked high behind the cash register. Terry Sue and I wandered around the aisles. She paused in front of a shelf of ceramic mugs, grinning at the animal pictures on each one, while I bought a roll of Kodak 620 film for my camera.

"Do you want one of those mugs?" I asked and pulled down a white glazed one with a cocker spaniel decal on it. "Hetty gave me some money for your birthday." Terry Sue pressed her lips to the mug and gave the puppy decal a slobbery kiss. "I'm going to call him Joe," she said.

"Y'all have a nice day now," the saleslady said when we purchased it. She placed the mug in a square box and fastened the lid with a piece of scotch tape. Terry Sue and I walked across the parking lot and opened the back door of the car. She pulled the mug out of the box and put it on the seat.

"I love you, I love you, Joey," she said. "Promise, Linda Sue, you won't let anything happen to my new friend. He's so sweet."

"Okay," I said.

She waved goodbye to the mug. I pressed my fingers hard to my eyes so that Terry Sue wouldn't see that I was crying a bit. We went to find Mama and Papa who were still waiting in the DQ line.

The party for Terry Sue's thirteenth birthday at Johnson's Shut-Ins was a flop for a lot of reasons. The main reason was, we never got anywhere near the shut-ins. Before we'd left home in the morning, I had read the description of the famous Johnson's Water Park in the *World Book Encyclopedia*. Tilya said the *World Book* was for dummies. She was wrong. You had to be pretty smart to understand their description of hot volcanic ash forming a narrow channel on the east fork of the Black River over a billions of years ago. I wasn't smart enough. I needed to see the chutes with water flowing down them, like in the *World Book* photo. I needed to jump from the cliffs into the gorges with my legs tucked into a cannonball dive. That's what the kids in the picture were doing. But on the day of Terry Sue's birthday party, not one Berk went close to the chutes and gorges at Johnson's Shut-Ins. Our bathing suits stayed packed in the draw-string bag we brought them in. Every time one of us inched away from the picnic table to change into a bathing suit in the restroom, Mama said, "*Carefu.*" I think that meant be careful and we had no business being at a waterfall far from home. We might as well have stayed in University City and walked to Heman Park.

To make things worse, Papa hadn't brought a fishing rod, tackle box and pail of worms, like the other dads at the Shut-Ins. I guessed Chaim Rubenstein forgot to mention fishing. Papa sat at the table drinking a seltzer and reading the *Post Dispatch,* the only man I saw wearing long khaki shorts and leather shoes with socks pulled high above his calves. The sound of children jumping from the rocks into those ancient pools of water reached us through the trees.

Mama said, "The *kinder*. You should only know what happened to the *kinder*."

"What children, Mama?" I hoped and prayed that the three

boys standing on the picnic table next to ours hadn't overheard her way of speaking English. I stood behind Terry Sue so that they couldn't get a full view of her. They seemed too busy spritzing each other with water guns to notice us.

"In Lodz," she said, smoothing the folds in the plastic table covering brought from home.

She sank the candles into the birthday cake that Hetty made for Terry Sue. When we sang "Happy Birthday," our voices were low and somber, more like a dirge than a celebration.

Hetty presented Terry Sue with the family gift. It was nothing big, just a white cotton pullover with the price tag still hanging from the sleeve. Short sleeves. A Peter Pan collar in a criss-crossed Tartan pattern, like one of those plaids from Scotland. Terry Sue immediately slid it over her head, straining to see something embroidered in yellow thread above the pocket.

"Yellow?" Mama said. "Like on your coats."

Hetty glared at her. "Mama, please."

"It's a happy colour, yellow," Tilya said.

Terry Sue bubbled with glee. She vowed to wear her new top until the day she died.

Papa poked his head over the newspaper to see the monogram initials stitched on Terry Sue's shirt. He nodded in approval, but I was too embarrassed to concentrate on the shirt or the yellow stitching or my family. My eyes focused on Terry Sue who was tearing the crusts from her chopped egg sandwich. Underneath the picnic table, next to her foot, I saw half of the sandwich lying on the ground. Ants swarmed the white bread. I started to hum the only song I knew about ants. I'd learned it in kindergarten. Our teacher, Mrs. O'Hagan, would have all the children march in a circle while singing this song about ants marching down to the ground to get out of the rain. She seemed to love that song. We'd practice it at least once a week, swinging our arms and stomping our feet, some of us holding tambourines and bells that we shook in time to the music. Our small voices were always strong and happy in the beginning of the song, so sure that the ants would triumph over whatever happened along the way. But with each verse, we became less sure. Our voices became lower. We stopped shaking the musical instruments. Then someone would drop to the floor. That was the part of the song that scared me.

I reached for my Brownie Hawkeye on the picnic bench and snapped a picture of Terry Sue's ant sandwich. Then I took another picture of the sandwich and her foot without a sandal and another one of just her blue and white sandal with cross straps lying sideways on the ground. I didn't know how or when the sandal came loose and fell off. I couldn't take my eyes away from the troubling things happening to her.

May 12, 1962

Dear baby sis (she wrote to me from the Missouri State Mental Hospital),

What a beautiful spring morning for my 16th birthday. I think I'll take a walk outside if Head Nurse will let me out of this lunatic asylum for ten minutes. (That's what they used to call this place in the olden days, you know, but I just call it The Mental.) It was one thing to be a patient in Renard Hospital with kids my own age, but now I feel like I'm an inmate in a prison. The ward here is filled with strange people. A lot of them are older than me. They look like they've been here for years, maybe their whole lives, and they're not going anywhere. I might be here my whole life, too, and. I'm just turning 16.

Did you know, Linda Sue, that I always wanted to have a sweet sixteen party with a cake to celebrate the big day? One

of those white square cakes from the bakery with pink roses and writing on it. Isn't it funny that my sixteenth birthday falls on a Saturday? It's just perfect for a girl and boy party with dancing real close, like Tilya and Robby sometimes used to do behind our house. I saw them kissing once. I was hiding under the kitchen window where they couldn't see me, and holding my breath. If you can keep a secret, it was more than dancing and kissing. I think it was S-E-X. Have you ever been kissed? I hope Cuddles comes to see me for my birthday. That's not his real name, but I call him that because he's so round, like a teddy bear. He's one of the young social workers who likes to play monopoly with me. I'm dying to kiss him. Our hands touched the other day when he passed me the Get Out of Jail Free card. I nearly had a heart attack. The side of his palm felt so cool and smooth. Well, kind of clammy. I noticed that his knuckles have little black hairs growing on them. I don't think Papa has hair on his knuckles, does he? Please check for me so I can tell Cuddles the next time I see him. Maybe he'll tell me why I'm here.

   I haven't gotten any birthday cards from the family. HN says that she's keeping them all until I gain 2 pounds. That meanie. So I made a card for myself at the craft table on Thursday and wrote this little poem.

Every girl dreams of this day
I remember when I was little and used to play
But now that I'm sixteen, I'm on my way
To a very bright future. What more can I say?

I heard that turning sixteen can be really great.
You can drive a car for goodness sake.
So I'm going to blow out the candles on my cake
And make a wish to have a date.

Do you think Cuddles will ask me for a real date? I decorated the outside of the card with purple tulips. I love anything purple.

Love ya bushels full.

XOXO, Terry Sue

Five

I WATCHED THE BLADES of the antique-looking fan turn overhead, feeling woozy and scared that it would fall from the ceiling. Every creak of the motor made me tremble. Maybe it would be death by decapitation, like the guillotine in the French Revolution. Someone at school said the head remains conscious for a while after it is separated from the body. Mama would kill herself if the fan fell and decapitated us. Terry Sue, wrapped in one of those green hospital gowns, lay in the bed next to me, eyes closed, breathing heavily, her dinner of fried chicken and mashed potatoes untouched. The smell of grease and gravy, the thick as paste kind, turned my stomach. Where was her new top with the yellow embroidered letters on it, I wondered. Hetty was going to be really mad if Terry Sue lost her brand new pullover already.

Outside our hospital room, I overheard adults talking. One man was saying that the driver of a Pontiac Delux had fallen asleep at the wheel.

"Just up here on northbound 67 at Myers Road," he said. "Two cars were stopped at the lights. Must have been about four o'clock." A cart clattered along the hospital corridor. I shifted in bed, turning my ear in the direction of the door.

A different voice, a woman's voice, described the trunks of the rear-ended cars. "Smashed to smithereens," she said in a mid-western drawl. I tried to visualize smithereens, but it all seemed too unbelievable. "One was an old Plymouth, the other a Ford." I remembered none of it.

I looked across at Terry Sue in a deep sleep, aware now that her face was bruised around the eyes and her nose was swollen out of shape. Staring out the window, I saw the branches of the giant elm trees, which seemed like the extended limbs of a monster. When I tried to stretch my arms, I felt a jolt of pain. My left shoulder and upper arm wouldn't move. I dreaded delivering the news to Terry Sue that her mug with Joe the cocker spaniel on it had probably splintered into a million tiny bits of clay.

"Sorry, kiddo," I whispered into the space separating our hospital beds. She moaned. I felt so guilty that I had let her new friend Joey die. What kind of a sister promises to protect a dog on a mug then doesn't? I felt like I should say more than sorry kiddo. I felt like I should try to save her life.

"Terry Sue," I said. "You've got to get better. If there's a secret living inside of you, something we can't see, tell me. I need to know what's wrong with you so I can figure out how not to lose you."

Once we were home, Papa spoiled us with heavenly hash, bon bon creams, and marshmallow eggs from the best chocolate maker in St. Louis. Even the satin boxes with Mavrakos scripted elegantly across the top looked expensive. And we were allowed to sample a piece, then return it to its pleated wrapper or spit the sugary goop into our hands. The nibbled chocolates looked as if an army of mice had ransacked the boxes strewn everywhere. Only Lenny, our future orthodontist and brother-in-law, seemed concerned. Sometimes he mentioned the word cavity, apologetically. Mama spent her days pampering us, always with a frightened look in her almond shaped eyes, as if there was something beyond my fractured collarbone and Terry Sue's broken nose that terrified her. Arrangements for Hetty's wedding at Beth Israel in June came to a halt.

"How can I think about a wedding when two of my children are still in the woods?" Mama said over and over while cursing Chaim Rubenstein and his crazy suggestion that we should go to Johnson's Shut-Ins. The wedding was postponed until August and Mama began to make meals again. Every night she prepared dinners of chicken soup with rice, roasted chicken, potatoes and carrots. Broccoli, which might possibly have a bug hiding in one of the florets, never touched our plates. Terry Sue pushed the food around with her fork, but refused to swallow a whole mouthful, resisting even the watery soup.

Hetty once asked Terry Sue why she wasn't combing her hair more often and the truth was if she brushed it too much, some would fall out. Blonde strands frequently covered her shoulders.

Lenny showered us with so many stuffed animals that before long we seemed to be living in a velveteen zoo of pandas, elephants, monkeys, ponies, penguins, and an off-season Easter bunny. The entire collection rested on a shelf by Terry Sue's bed where she devoted hours to their care and feeding — mostly stale bon bons — except for the unicorn.

"I never saw a unicorn in the St. Louis zoo," I said when Lenny presented it to us on a Sunday about three weeks after the car crash.

"That's because they don't exist," he said.

"Then why did you buy us one?" He took some time to think about it, scratched his crotch, but didn't come up with a single word.

For a week the plush white animal with pink ears and a single horn jutting from its forehead sat alone on the living room carpet among discarded newspapers and back issues of *Life* magazine. A complete mess. Just by accident I caught Terry

Sue with a knife in her hand one afternoon in mid-June. She was about to slice off the unicorn's little horn.

"It's having an operation," she said. "To make it feel less freakish"

"You're using mother's kosher knife?"

"Now it's an ordinary horse," she said when the job was done. The stuffing from the unicorn fell, like a light summer drizzle, to the floor.

A few minutes later Robby Sloan arrived at our house, reeking of cigarette smoke and wearing a ripped and faded T-shirt that was much too big for him. A green canvas sack swung from his shoulder. The damaged unicorn caught his eye.

"Tennessee Williams would love that," he said glancing at the fragile animal. "It reminds me of his play *The Glass Menagerie*."

"Is that a kid's story?" I was getting tired of the way Robby always mentioned plays we never heard of.

A smirk crossed his face. "Sort of," he said as he turned toward me. "Tennessee Williams went to University City High, you know."

His eyes focused directly on my chest where my folded arm was resting in a sling. I felt a small tingle inside my blouse and left the room to get a drink of water.

"*Nu*," Mama said when Robby left our house. "A nice boy, but why can't he comb his hair?" She pulled a cookie sheet from the oven with a quilted potholder so worn that her face twitched as the heat touched her hand.

"Is that ALL you care about?" Tilya said. The poppy seed cookies came out of the oven perfectly crispy and golden around the edges. I think Mama carried the recipe around in her head because I never saw her open *The Joy of Cooking* to make them.

"Okay," Hetty said. "Tell us. Is Robby Sloan Jewish?"

"His mother is Jewish," Tilya said. She hesitated before dropping the A-bomb. "But..."

"There's a 'but'?" Mama said. She scraped a few remaining crumbs off the baking sheet with a spatula before sliding a second batch into the oven.

"They're atheists, Mama. And guess what else."

"More I need?" It sounded like something was stuck in her throat, a hard clump of fear that she couldn't swallow.

"Mama, you forgot the orange rind in the *mohn* cookies," Hetty complained.

"So," Mama said as she joined us at the kitchen table. "Do you think we had orange rinds in the *shtetl*? You'd be lucky to have an orange once in a blue moon."

Tilya rattled off the Sloan family details. "His mother works. Every day. Out of the house. At Washington University. And so does his father." The overheated room suddenly smelled smoky from burning cookie dough. Tilya continued, "His mother is a geneticist with three kids and they have a dog called Gregor Mendel."

"Gregor Mendel? This is a name for a dog?" Mama tossed the ruined cookies into the garbage. "Maybe the dog should be Dracula."

"You know, he was the founder of genetics." Tilya said.

"Who named their kid Gregor Mendel?" Terry Sue said. She picked up the last edible cookie from the table, sniffed it, and dropped it into her pocket.

"Gregor Mendel is Robby's dog. Weren't you listening?" Tilya stood up. "And his mother doesn't shave her legs or armpits."

"Gross." Terry Sue said.

"What does a geneticist do?" I said, lifting up my good arm, the one not in a sling. I tickled my armpit to feel if I had any hair growing there yet. I wished that Robby would spend more time at our house. I liked his red striped socks.

November 29, 1962

Dear Linda Sue (she wrote to me from the Missouri State Mental Hospital),

I've been here almost a half a year now and gained not one dumb pound in this dumb place. I'm scared to tell you how many I lost. The only thing that is good about The Mental is Cuddles who still comes to play Monopoly with me. He was able to get some mosaic tiles for me to make a flower for you, but I decided to surprise Mama and Papa with a present for their anniversary instead. Head Nurse found a small table in the storage closet and she's letting me decorate the whole top of it. But it has one wobbly leg.

You know that test I mentioned, the one my new doctor, Dr. Richardson, did on me a while ago. He didn't say exactly what was wrong, but he gave me pills to start my periods. Then he had a meeting with Mama, Papa, and me the other day. (I don't know if they told you about it.) But he said that I would always be short. It has something to do with chromosomes. I don't understand anything about chromosomes. Dr. Richardson tried to explain what chromosomes are. He even drew a picture with Xs and Ys, but honestly, I didn't understand a word he was saying. I just listened, feeling really freakish. I'm pretty sure that Mama and Papa didn't understand either. Why would they? Did anyone in Lodz ever talk about chromosomes? Well, Mama did start to cry and Papa tried to comfort her while I sat in a chair across the room. Anyway, I'm really going to eat more and try to grow taller. Miss you more than ever.

Lots of love, Terry Sue

P.S. *I'm enclosing the drawing Dr. Richardson made to explain chromosomes. Maybe you can show it to Tilya. She'll be able to figure it out because she's very smart and the one person in our family who is in university. You know science was never my best subject. Was it yours? I wish that Tilya would become a real doctor so that she could explain all of this to me, or a geneticist, like Robby's mother, who never shaved under her arms. Do you ever feel like a monster? I sometime do, but Dr. Richardson says that's because I'm not finished developing yet.*

    XOXO, *Terry Sue*

Six

THE ADMIRAL, I LEARNED from a pamphlet circulated at school, had five decks. It could carry four thousand passengers on its excursions up and down the Mississippi. I brought the riverboat advertisement home and read "Flashes from the Flagship S.S. Admiral" to everyone at dinner:

> *Dancing and romancing in the Blue Salon. Cocktails in the swank Club Admiral. Cool air like springtime in the mountains.... Gay umbrellas on the Lido Deck.... You're in for a circus on the Main Deck. Ahoy!*

"Can I go?" I asked Mama and Papa. "Everyone is going, even Fruma, and it's on the last day of school." We were eating bland borscht with sour cream to keep cool. Papa had a theory that it was better to eat spicy food in hot weather because it chilled the body, but Mama disagreed.

"It's a big deal to go on the Admiral," Tilya said. "Who doesn't know that?"

"Is the Admiral really as long as a city block?" I took Terry Sue's question as a sign of interest, proof that life was returning to her. For another thing, she scrunched her nose, which no longer appeared swollen. She looked almost normal.

"Do you want to go with me, Terry Sue? We could bring lots of Coppertone so your skin doesn't burn." I thought about the hat she'd have to wear to protect her scalp from the sun and from the stares of passengers. "And my Brownie Hawkeye."

She said, "Maybe."

"Only if an adult goes with you," Papa said. True confession: if either one of my parents got anywhere near the bus taking us to the riverfront, I'd throw myself under the wheels.

Tilya said, "I'll go. The semester is done at Washington U." She smiled over her copy of *The Communist Manifesto* by someone named Karl Marx, which she was re-reading at the kitchen table. "But only if Robby comes with me."

"I didn't think the two of you would be caught dead on the Admiral," Hetty said. Nobody in our family fully understood Tilya. In her final year of high school, she had switched from the stylish crowd with bouffant hair and varsity letter sweaters to the clique that hated sports, wore old sandals (with socks) in the winter, and let their hair grow long and totally wild. Hetty said that Tilya's makeover was, like everything else in America, all about opportunity. After Tilya had failed twice to become a cheerleader, she joined The Brains and fell in love with Karl Marx. Well, he was more like an uncle.

"What do you actually do on the Admiral?" Terry Sue said.

"You have fun," Hetty said. She and Lenny sometimes took a cruise on warm weekend evenings. Once they got on the Admiral at midnight. "What you never do," she said, "is wear blue jeans."

The day before the school excursion, Hetty ironed a cotton dress for me and coaxed Terry Sue into going on the Admiral with an offer of fake pearls. Mama pulled a tangled bra from the laundry basket and gave it to me.

"Here," she said, "If you don't wear this, you're not going tomorrow."

"What about Terry Sue?" I asked.

"You're not your sister's keeper," she said. "And some day,

you'll thank me when your bosoms don't mop the floor."

I fiddled with the metal hooks on the bra until Mama became more interested in her African violet sitting on the stereo console cabinet. White spots covered the plant's leaves. The dark wood of the cabinet showed water damage, too. I pretended not to see it.

Cobblestone streets stretched along the banks of the Mississippi. "This here is Laclede's Landing," the bus driver called out, "where St. Louis began, way back when." No one seemed to be listening, including Tilya and Robby who sat in front of Terry Sue and me, their heads touching. It looked like they had drifted together on purpose.

I tapped Tilya on the shoulder. "Could you be quiet so I can hear what he's saying?"

"It was a trading post then," the driver said. "Last stop for those wantin' to tame the western frontier."

Outside, the old warehouses and saloons were boarded up. "Yup, a riverboat community lived and worked here. A thrivin' one it was ... once."

Through the bus window, between deserted buildings, I saw the Mississippi for the first time — muddy, brown, slow moving and not very wide. This can't be it, I said to myself. Maybe the Mississippi River was mightier in the state of Mississippi. A hot wind swept across our faces as we walked toward the gangplank of the Admiral. Piped music filled the air. Terry Sue tucked her hands under her sun hat to cover her ears.

"That's the steam calliope on the Admiral," Robby said. "My grandpa once made a calliope out of car horns and hubcaps. Always reminds me of a whorehouse."

"It reminds me of the organ grinder at a circus and cotton candy," Tilya said. Her polka dot dress flew above her knees.

"Look, there's the captain," Terry Sue said, pinching my arm while pointing to a man standing close to the paddle wheel. He wore an official white hat with SS Admiral on it.

We followed Tilya and Robby up the staircase to the second deck of the Admiral. When we shoved open the padded doors, it felt like we were stepping into an ice box.

"What happened to all the hot air?" Terry Sue said.

A boy pushed in front of us. Over his shoulder he said, "They conditioned it."

Tilya and Robby were already on the dance floor. I squished behind one of the pillars to watch them, her curvy body pressed to his puny chest, his hand resting on her back, like he owned her. I snapped the button of my camera. As soon as Tilya caught me taking pictures of her and Robby with their cheeks all flushed from squeezing them together, she scowled at me.

"Get lost." She mouthed the words several times. I knew she was serious because her eyes turned into angry slits and her lips tightened into a straight line. I pointed the camera at Terry Sue. Through the viewfinder, I saw her hatless, eyes wide open. For once, she looked happy.

"Hold your horses," I said to her as we entered the arcade on the main deck. Pinging sounds jumped at us. Boys, huddled over pinball machines, shook the coin-eaters from side to side. "I feel sick," I said to Terry Sue. "Like I'm going to vomit."

She blinked. "Here?"

We stopped in front of a booth where a bear darted between clumps of trees. For a minute, I believed the animal was real. The object of the game, someone said, was to shoot the grizzly bear. A blond in the crowd, no more than seven years old with straight-across bangs, picked up a rifle from the stand nearby, took aim and fired. Around him kids shouted "killkillkillkill."

I rested my chin in the wisps of Terry Sue's hair, the little that was left of it. She was two years older than I was, but a whole head shorter. The fuzz on her scalp felt safe in a familiar sort of way. I When I peeked at the bear, it was standing on its hind legs, howling. Blood splattered from the bear's mouth.

"I think I'm going to vomit," I said again. We walked toward a fortune teller with olive skin, a beard, and long earrings drooping from his turban to his shoulders.

"Why does he have a rag wrapped around his head?" Terry Sue asked. She stepped away from the booth.

"Because he's the Mystic Swami. Can't you read?"

"I don't want to have my fortune told," Terry Sue said. She stared at the crystal ball in the swami's hands. "I'm too afraid."

"So am I."

On the Lido deck, high above the water, I gazed at the barges moving cargo down the Mississippi. The river didn't seem like an old man to me, not like Moses in the bible or my uncle Herman who mother always said looked good for his age. He was sixty-seven and bald, but he usually wore a skull cap which covered the shiny top of his head. Mama and Papa would not understand this river, I thought, not in the way that whoever wrote the song about it did. Our parents seemed to be the opposite of the Mississippi, though I couldn't say exactly how. I held still, letting the dark water roll through me while Terry Sue smothered her arms with more Coppertone.

Tilya was smoking alone when we found her on the side of the dance floor. I could tell that she had been crying.

"Why don't you get Mama and Papa a souvenir with the money they gave you," she said. Sniffles dripped from her nose although she didn't have an allergy. "Maybe a snow globe or a giant pencil or a captain's hat. They'd love anything you bought for them. Just go."

It was Terry Sue who found the lucky charm machine that stamped out a silver life preserver about the size of a half dollar. On one side it read "SS Admiral" and the other side it had a cloverleaf with the words "May God hold you in the palm of his hand" engraved around it in small cursive letters. "What's that supposed to mean?" I said. My head ached from the jolt of noise and light illuminating the arcade.

"How should I know," Terry Sue said, stuffing the life preserver into her purse. It joined the chewed gum she already dropped in there.

"I think it's about being saved if the boat sinks," I said. I began to worry about Tilya crying on the side of the dance floor upstairs and going to look for Robby.

"You mean if this boat sinks?"

"No," I said. "I was thinking about the boat that brought Hetty and Tilya to America. What if it had sunk?"

"It didn't," she said.

"It could have," I said.

"Then we wouldn't exist and you wouldn't have to worry about me."

Robby swayed his hips to the music on the second floor. He seemed unconcerned about Tilya's sadness, or at least that's how he appeared to me when Terry Sue and I bumped into him in the Blue Salon ballroom. It didn't take him more than one minute to invite me to dance. He pulled me in close, the same way he danced with Tilya, but the top of my head only reached his chest. I hoped she wasn't watching us from somewhere. Why was she crying, anyway? I held my breath to block the stale smell of his cigarettes. Then I started counting the number of couples on the dance floor. When I got bored, I squeezed my eyes shut and thought about baby Moses floating in the bulrushes of the Nile. It was a good thing that his sister Miriam helped to save him. Robby took my hand, lifted it over my head and twirled me around once. I felt kind of dizzy and excited and scared. I didn't know what I felt. Before he had a chance to twirl me again, I wiggled my hand free and sprinted up the stairs to the ladies' room.

On the swinging door to the bathroom I saw the name Sonja Henie. Who would name a bathroom after a figure skater, I wondered. Locked inside the bathroom stall, I felt safe. Sitting on the toilet seat, I began to daydream about becoming an Olympic skating star myself, making my sisters so proud — and jealous. Then I noticed several spots of blood in the cotton crotch of my underpants. Confused at first by the stain, I made a quick decision to tell no one. And Mama would be the last to know. For Terry Sue's sake, maybe I'd never tell her. Mama often prayed aloud in the kitchen, especially when she was chopping carrots and onions, that Terry Sue should only be blessed with regular periods. "Without pills, dear *got*," I'd hear her whisper, "and before Linda Sue gets hers."

I folded a hunk of toilet paper into a rectangle and placed it over the spots in my underwear. I could ditch the evidence later. Returning to the second floor to find Tilya and Terry Sue, I remember passing a bank of large windows that I hadn't noticed before. I stood there for a long time, looking at the big river flowing like a ribbon as far as I could see.

February 17, 1963

Dearest baby sis (she wrote to me from the Missouri State Mental Hospital),

Please don't tell Mama and Papa, Linda Sue, but Dr. Richardson just told me that my heart, lungs, or kidneys could give out at any moment. He's threatening to hook me up to an IV if I don't gain weight very soon. I really don't want to think about it now. It's so cold in here and all I want to do is remember the fun times we had together.

Don't you remember how much fun we had cramming into that photo booth on the Admiral? It was on the first deck, I think, with all those games and stuff that made you nauseous.

You had to swivel the seat up in the photo booth so that my face wasn't cut in half. There wasn't a speck of space between us in that booth. How could there be? We were so squished onto the seat made for one, smiling our prettiest ... FLASH ... making rabbit ears ... FLASH ... sticking out our tongues ... FLASH . Don't you just love how the pictures come out in a long strip from that machine? Remember how you were wearing a bra for the first time? (Don't worry, you can't see it in the pictures.) And you kept complaining that it was riding up your back. I happened to be in the room when mother said that you had to wear the bra or your breasts would mop the floor. There, I've said it: Breasts. Breasts. Breasts. She wouldn't use the real word for any female body part. But, you know, I can't forget that she said that to you because she never said anything about breasts or bosoms to me. I was so envious I wanted to strangle you that day.

Pretty please, Linda Sue, I trust you and only you to keep those pictures in a safe place for me. I can't keep them here by my bed because you never know what's going to happen to things in this place. The other day my roommate noticed that her high school class ring, which she stored in the drawer of her night table, had disappeared. I kid you not. Now who would want a ring with the name Kelly Fishman engraved on it? Just don't tell me that you hate those photos. And please don't destroy them. Never, ever.

Love ya always. Terry Sue

P.S. I promise not to tell Mama that you hid your stained underpants in the back of the closet so that she wouldn't know when you got your first period. Lucky you. I wish I had your chromosomes or whatever makes you get your period without taking silly pills.

Love again, T.S.

Seven

WE WALKED THE TWENTY-FIVE BLOCKS from our house on Tulane to the Delmar Loop, the pavement still burning from the afternoon heat. Sweat trickled down my face like a slow-drip ice cream cone.

"It's hotter than Hades," Hetty said.

Tilya said, "It's July, for God's sakes and why don't you say what you really mean. It's hotter than hell." She had removed her sandals once we were out of Mama's sight and slipped them into a grungy green knapsack slung over her shoulder. "Why does everyone in this family always try to cover things up?"

To prevent the bottoms of her feet from blistering, Tilya hopped from one lawn to the next. (Mama always warned that she would end up with Hoof and Mouth disease from walking outside with bare feet.) I tried to follow, but my legs, which were very long (the kids at school nicknamed me daddy longlegs), couldn't keep up with hers.

"Hurry up," Hetty said. She was less than thrilled to be saddled with me on a Friday night.

"And if you don't do what we say," Tilya said, "big men wearing tall, heavy boots are going to get you." Their eyes locked in one of those private moments they sometimes shared, times when I felt completely left out. Then Tilya poked me so hard at the waist that I nearly tumbled on the grass.

"If you push me like that again," I said, annoyed with her

gruffness, "I'm going to fall down and break another bone. I'll need a sling on my arm again." That I didn't need, I thought, with Hetty's wedding back on track.

"Leiba Shayndel, will you hurry up already?" Hetty said to me. She was meeting Lenny in front of the Tivoli to see a movie about a young girl in Paris named Gigi who acted like a tomboy.

"I'm not Leiba Shayndel. And don't call me by my Yiddish name. I'm Linda Sue," I said, reminding her, whenever I could, that I was born in America and I had an American name, just the same as Terry Sue did.

Every kid in U. City wanted to be seen in the Delmar Loop on Friday nights, hanging out at Joe's Billiards or eating *treif* pepperoni pizza at Cicero's. Tilya once confessed that the bacon pizza was much better than the pepperoni because the fried bacon was crispier than the soggy round pieces of pepperoni.

"Can I get a Cherry Coke before the movie?" I asked. I loved the soda fountain in the drugstore on the corner of Delmar and Enright. I'd twirl around on the cushioned stools while the guy behind the counter pumped syrup into a glass and then added fizzy water to it. The best part was when the Cherry Coke arrived with a long straw. I'd lean over the glass and slurp slowly, sometimes swishing the soda around in my mouth to make it last longer. We never had straws at our house. Mama feared we'd poke our eyes out with the sharp edges. And, besides, nobody in Lodz used purple and blue plastic straws to drink anything.

"Pretty please, Hetty. I'll be good the rest of the night."

"Maybe," said Hetty.

We passed the huge stone lions flanking Delmar close to the public library. Tilya pointed to an area of large homes on the south side of the street. "Robby lives over there on Waterman," she said. "Not far from Wash U." Her voice hummed with familiarity, almost as if she lived around here, too, and our parents were also professors at the university.

"You mean, close to Beth Israel?" Hetty said. "There are some gorgeous older homes around there."

"I can guarantee you that the Sloan family doesn't care whether they live close to Beth Israel or not," Tilya said. "And you are becoming more and more like Mama every day." They linked arms with me, lifting my feet off the ground, as we crossed into the commercial section of the Loop.

"That's where we lived when we first arrived in St. Louis," Hetty said when we came to Eastgate Avenue. "In a one bedroom apartment over there." The three-storey building they had lived in was located just a half a block from Delmar. On both sides of the street, apartments were crammed together, the brick wall of one building nearly touching the building next to it. Heaps of dirt and weeds covered the front yards.

"Does the Loop look like Lodz?" I turned to Hetty and then to Tilya, wishing that for once they would say something about where our family lived before coming to the United States. Terry Sue and I had often asked them, but had gotten nowhere. Neither one answered.

A little further down Delmar on Leland, we bumped into Ellen Brownstein. I knew for a fact that Terry Sue would have traded anything, even that mangled unicorn of hers, to be invited to Ellen Brownstein's house for a swim.

"Where's Terry Sue tonight?" she asked us. Her arms and legs were a bronze colour, more orange than tan, which clashed with the red nail polish on her fingers and toes. Freckles dotted her nose. "Your sister is just so adorable. Why isn't she with you?"

I despised Ellen Brownstein for the way she treated Terry Sue. She had some nerve to tell us that Terry Sue was adorable when she never called her, never went bike riding with her, never included her in pool parties, never wanted her as a friend.

A few weeks back, I had decided that Terry Sue and I would drop by Ellen Brownstein's house in the well-to-do section of University City. Maybe our visit would get something started between Terry Sue and her. Mama and Papa were at their weekly Canasta game that night. At seven o'clock, it was still light outdoors and the thermometer on the living room wall read ninety-three degrees.

"Let's get out of here," I had said. "Don't you want to go find Ellen?" We laced up our sneakers, wheeled our Schwinns from the garage, and cycled up to Gannon and then as far west as Swarthmore. Terry Sue shouted ahead to me, "Are we going to be at Ellen's soon? I can't wait to surprise her." When we approached Mulberry Lane, a whiff of chlorine hit us. We left our bikes on the ground and scrambled through the underbrush. I twisted through the barbed wire fence bordering the Brownstein's backyard, Terry Sue following, so excited to see a swimming pool that she had heard was the shape of a kidney, and to say hi to Ellen.

"Where's Ellen?" she said as we got closer to the chlorine smell. "I thought you said we were going to find Ellen."

"We will," I said. Warm liquid dripped down my arm. I looked over at Terry Sue. Her shoulder had a hole bulging with blood from the barbed wire fence just like mine.

We crawled close enough to spy on Ellen and two other girls lounging on the patio. We could hear the ice cubes clinking in their frosted glasses. They were sipping pink lemonade with brightly coloured straws and having a great time. I thought about running over to all three of them and grabbing those straws from their glasses, jabbing them into their giggling eyes and blinding them so they could know what it felt like not to be perfect. But that just seemed like a stupid idea because Ellen would probably still find some way to avoid being Terry Sue's friend.

Now, on the corner of Delmar and Leland Avenue, Hetty said to Ellen. "Oh, Terry Sue had a date tonight. She's so popular, you know."

I knew Hetty was lying. The truth was, Terry Sue didn't want to come to the movies with us. She'd claimed to be uninterested in a musical about a tomboy who lived in Paris, even when Hetty had told her that Gigi was also a debutante who wore fancy hats and flouncy dresses. Lying on her bed surrounded by her stuffed animals, Terry Sue hadn't moved or talked, as if she had entered a private world where debutantes, movies, and people didn't matter anymore. I'd tried to tickle her out of it. It hadn't worked.

At the Tivoli, the Friday night crowd crushed oversized drink cups under seats and spit on the floor. The theatre smelled sleazy and damp. Just as the newsreel began, an older girl sitting next to me tapped my elbow.

"Excuse me," she said. "I hate to bother you, but do you mind if I go to the bathroom?" I was sitting with one leg tucked under me, settled in my seat, expecting to see Buckingham Palace or the Boulder Dam or Bob Hope who was always entertaining American troops overseas. The voice in the newsreel boomed, "Science on the march."

The older girl began to scoot over me, stopping to apologize twice for stepping on my toe. Her bum blocked my entire view of the screen.

The voice in the newsreel was listing all the great scientific discoveries that had happened so far in the 1950s. "In the field of medicine," the voice said, "a vaccine for polio, the most vicious disease of our era, has been discovered, due to the pioneering research of Dr. Jonas Salk." At the mention of Salk, my chest puffed up. I knew that Papa admired Jonas Salk and wanted at least one of his daughters to be like him. If our family believed in heroes — which we absolutely did — Salk was way up there with Henrietta Szold. "You see," Papa would say to us, "what a Jew with immigrant parents like yours can do. You see how Salk found a cure." I moved my head from side to side to see around the older girl's bum. I was thinking about what Papa said about Salk. I was thinking about Salk's next cure and how maybe he could find a cure for something that wasn't the most horrible disease of the century but was killing Terry Sue.

As soon as the girl passed over me, I saw fuzzy blobs swelling and separating from each other on the screen. The voice proclaimed the birth of a new field of science: human genetics.

I turned to Hetty who was holding hands with Lenny. "Hetty," I whispered. "Doesn't Robby's mother have something to do with genetics?"

"Shush," she admonished, pretending to zip her mouth shut and throw away the key on the slimy floor.

"Don't you remember? His dog is named Gregor Mendel?"

The blobs continued to squiggle across the screen. "Now we know that normal human cells have forty six chromosomes, not forty-eight." I didn't know what he was talking about.

"Hetty," I said. "I don't understand what a chromosome is."

"Neither do I, so shut up."

"Ask Lenny. He's going to be an orthodontist."

"Shut up."

"I want to know what a chromosome is."

"He'll tell you later."

"I want to know now."

Lenny leaned over, his head practically touching Hetty's boobs. "It's like a blueprint."

Sitting at the Tivoli in the dark, I felt confused. If Tilya were here, she could explain chromosomes in a jiffy. Words like cells and DNA and molecules and nucleus meant nothing to me. Papa could forget about me becoming the next Jonas Salk. I couldn't possibly be a scientist or a doctor. My brain didn't think that way. And at the moment, I was more concerned that Tilya was with Robby at the Varsity up the street watching a film about three Russian brothers with a name I couldn't pronounce. I was green-eyed with jealousy. She was probably holding hands with Robby.

March 22, 1963

Dearest oldest sister (she wrote to Hetty from the Missouri State Mental Hospital),

You've got to get me out of here. I have been at this crazy place for months and I still don't know where it is. The building is high on a hill on a street called Arsenal. But where is that? I bet you know and can come to get me because you are my oldest sister and you know St. Louis better than the rest of us. I feel so far away from you and the family and University City. Also, I'm bored to death with jigsaw puzzles. At least Cuddles, the cute social worker, stops by pretty often to play Monopoly with me. I guess he's got a lot of time on his hands. He's always surprised that I can count my money and buy houses and hotels for my properties. (I still go for Marvin Gardens the first time I land on it.)

I'm really trying to eat, but it would be a lot easier if the food here didn't taste like garbage. I was never a big fan of biscuits. Remember those ones that came out of the yellow Betty Crocker Bisquick box. So light and tender like a happy heart. Here the biscuits have bits of bacon in them, which I think they add before the buttermilk. I remember Mama used to make mandelbrot, *those long cookies that were so hard you could break your teeth on them. She had to put them in the oven twice. The first time she baked them in a loaf and then she'd slice them in the pan, sprinkle them with* cinnamon and sugar, then brown them again. I miss Mama.

Can you believe that I still have that little fleshy scar that Linda Sue and I got the night we tried to find Ellen Brownstein's swimming pool? (Mama never figured out how we got those scars.) I hope the scar never goes away. It's forever, just like me and you and everyone in our family. You know that I always wanted to be Ellen Brownstein's best friend and go swimming at her house, like all the popular girls. If I ever get out of here, maybe Linda Sue and I can spy on her pool again. Write me soon.

Love ya tons and tons, Terry Sue

P.S. When you come to get me in The Mental, remember that the door to this ward is always locked. I feel like a prisoner but I haven't done anything wrong, have I?

More love, T.S.

Eight

THREE NIGHTS BEFORE Hetty's wedding at Beth Israel, when she tried on her dress for Joyce Hirschfield and the zipper got stuck, a second unpredictable thing happened. It was worse than the car accident on the way home from Johnson's Shut-Ins.

The bad surprise started with Hetty sulking around the house in a grouchy mood. If Terry Sue or I dared to look at her cross-eyed, she'd have a fit. It seemed like a moat surrounded Hetty, not the kind filled with water circling a medieval castle, but a deep, dry ditch separating her from us. Maybe it was the heat or wedding jitters or worry about what to wear on her honeymoon. Bathing suits, short shorts, skirts, sun suits, dressy off-white slacks, underwear, nightgowns, a robe, and Kotex sanitary pads carpeted the floor of her room.

"If a burglar came through your window tonight," Joyce said, "he'd think another burglar had already been here." She jiggled Hetty's zipper, trying to pry the champagne coloured taffeta from the teeth of the zipper while Terry Sue and I watched her. I had a scary thought: Joyce was going to catch a piece of Hetty's back fat in the zipper. Scanning the piles of stuff Hetty had gathered for the honeymoon, Joyce straightened her spine and muttered, "What a dump."

Hetty puckered the corners of her mouth, as if she had eaten a sour lemon candy. I recognized the look on her face because our family had a word for it. She became *b'rogez*, which Papa said in English meant a person felt either angry or insulted. "You really think this is a dump?" she said, turning to Joyce.

"What's that flashlight doing over there?" Terry Sue said. "You and Lenny are going to a hotel in Chicago for four days." During the months leading up to the wedding, Terry Sue squeezed every romantic drop from the marriage arrangements. She wanted to know if Hetty and Lenny would French kiss on the altar and when Lenny planned to remove Hetty's garter. Now she picked up one of Hetty's lace bras from the floor, curving it around her flat chest, as if she were the sexy bride to be.

"Trust me, Joyce," Hetty said. She wrapped a stray lock of hair behind her ear. "My room in this house is luxurious."

"Compared to what? To Lodz?" I figured this was my last chance to press Hetty for the information about Lodz that she always guarded, protecting it in an airtight vault she seemed to carry with her. Only a couple of days left, I calculated, before Hetty would turn into someone else, leaving behind whatever had happened there, and become Mrs. Hetty Abrams, married American lady.

She smoothed her half zipped wedding dress over her hips. After a moment, Hetty said, "I can't tell you what happened. Tilya and I made a pact to keep everything a secret." Joyce continued to yank the zipper without making any progress until Hetty squirmed away from her. She reached under her bed and pulled out a dusty suitcase.

"Just say something, Hetty," I begged her. I imagined voices calling her name from inside the suitcase, dead cousins, school friends that may have disappeared, dolls she had adored and lost. "You don't have to tell us the whole *megillah* right now. And I swear that I'll never mention a single word to anyone, especially not to Tilya."

Terry Sue said, "My lips are sealed, too, Hetty. Cross my heart and hope to die, stick a needle in my eye." A crooked grin crossed my face. Everyone knew that Terry Sue and I were the biggest blabber mouths. Only a crazy person would trust us with private information, even it was about events that happened in a different country twenty years ago.

Joyce glared at the mounds of clothing Hetty had created on the floor, more clothes, she remarked, than anyone could wear in a month. Frustrated by the stuck zipper and the mess on the floor, she threw her hands into the air and slinked out of the bedroom. Terry Sue and I didn't budge.

The first sentence Hetty spoke about Lodz that night, the first inkling Terry Sue and I had of her life before she came to St. Louis, hit hard. She was looking at her empty suitcase, breathing heavily and sobbing. "We couldn't take anything with us into the ghetto." Terry Sue and I sat on her bed, staring into space while Hetty described what she, Mama and Papa left behind: a bookcase and all of her children's books, the dining room table and chairs, the baby dresses sewn for her by grandmother, her puppet named Binke, the boxes of dishes mother had packed, the photos of mother and father on their wedding day. "I was only five years old at the time so I don't remember much," she said. "Only holding Papa's hand when we walked into the ghetto so I didn't get trampled."

"Hetty," I said, "Didn't Mama bring those soup bowls from Poland, you know, the hand-painted ones we used for Hanukah?" I loved the gold and blue flowers dancing around the rims of those bowls. Every time I turned one over and read "Made in Poland" on the underside of it, I felt I was holding something that had been passed down to me from Mama and before that, from her mama and, before that, from her mama's mama. Sometimes I almost could smell the steam from their chicken soup rising.

"Yeah," Hetty said. "Those soup bowls were made in Poland, but I bought them for Mama here at Famous Barr. And don't tell her I told you. She owned nothing by the time we left there." It was one of those moments when the truth hurt more than all the untruths I held onto. I shut my eyes and put my hands over my ears. I wished Hetty wouldn't say another word so that I could still believe what I wanted to believe about Lodz.

"Wait," I said to her, "I have to pee."

When I returned from the bathroom, Hetty was telling Terry Sue about some sort of a book that Papa made up called The Berkowitz Guide to Surviving in the Lodz Ghetto. Terry Sue wanted to know if The Berkowitz Guide had pictures because she loved to draw, but Hetty told her that it didn't even have written words and it was better that way. The guide, as she described it, consisted of rules that the whole family memorized after they were forced to move into the Lodz ghetto, except for Tilya who was an infant around that time and couldn't memorize anything. "I think I still know about four or five of the rules," Hetty said. "Papa made them easy for us."

She opened the lid of her suitcase to begin packing for her honeymoon. The flashlight was the first item Hetty touched. She toggled the switch back and forth to make sure that the batteries worked. Then she pointed the flashlight's little pool of light at her face and started to recite what she remembered from The Berkowitz Guide to Surviving in the Lodz Ghetto. Her voice sounded normal enough, but she was gripping the flashlight so tightly that her knuckles turned white. Terry Sue and I huddled closer together on the bed.

"Rule #1: Always speak as softly as a washcloth."

I itched my head where a mosquito had bitten me. From what Hetty told us, they had to leave behind everything when they moved from their apartment in the centre of Lodz into the ghetto. Why, then, were Mama and Papa able to take washcloths with them? I remembered that we had two or three washcloths in our linen closet on Tulane, but I was almost positive that they were not from Poland. I hesitated a moment, fearful that I might say the wrong thing. "In Rule #1, did Papa mean a dry or wet washcloth?"

Hetty became quiet. She put the flashlight into the suitcase, unable to go any further. When she bent over, the zipper on her wedding dress made a z-z-z sound, like the teeth on the zipper were conducting business.

"What about soap?" Terry Sue said. I also wondered about that. Most of the time, washcloths were filled with lots of hot soapy water, but I didn't dare ask Hetty how they kept clean in the ghetto.

"Papa meant a dry washcloth," she said. "There was no running water in our apartment in the ghetto." I squeezed Terry Sue around the waist as hard as I could. Hetty described their one room, the double bed they shared, the lice in her hair.

"We had to be quiet, always very quiet," she said. The reason silence was important, Hetty explained, was on account of the German police who were posted in the ghetto. They raided families suspected of having valuable things. "They would say, 'Give us your diamonds,' even if you'd never seen a diamond. Then they could beat you until you were blue to get you to say where your valuables were hidden." I interlaced my fingers like I was praying. "Papa said that if we were quiet as washcloths, the German police would skip our apartment. They'd think we were all dead inside."

Hetty walked over to the window and stared at the patches of sunburned grass in the backyard. The evening light began to soften into a hazy darkness. I hoped that a shooting star would flash in the night sky and make Hetty forget the other rules in The Berkowitz Guide. She turned away from the window, picking up several silky nightgowns from the floor which she rolled into long thin strips. Lining the edges of the suitcase with them, she asked whether we wanted to hear father's Rule #2.

"No," I said.

Terry Sue said "Yes" louder.

"Rule #2: Never go to the toilet when you hear big boots in the building."

"But what if you really had to go very, very badly?" Terry Sue said.

"Then father told us to use the bucket that sat in the corner. He would dump it after the visitors left." When Hetty said the word visitors, she crunched two fingers on both hands in the air. I'd seen Tilya do that same finger crunching motion many times. She called it sign language. The fingers, she'd said, conveyed a meaning exactly opposite to the real meaning of the word.

"Those big boots in the building," I said to Terry Sue. "They weren't visitors coming for tea and cookies."

Hetty told us that the toilet was outside the apartment in the courtyard. They shared it with other families, and sometimes there were long line-ups to use it. In the wintertime, the toilet was filled to the brim with ice. Pee and BMs overflowed onto the ground around the toilet. "It was impossible," she said, "not to step in it."

"Enough, Hetty," I said. "I don't want to hear any more about the Lodz ghetto." I scooted off the bed, ready to run out of her room. But Hetty didn't seem to be listening. She searched the floor for the next items to be packed for her honeymoon.

"I think the longer clothes should go on the bottom of the suitcase, like my off-white pants, don't you?"

"Are you going to sleep in your wedding dress tonight?" Terry Sue asked. Hetty reached behind her back, grabbing the taffeta on either side of the zipper. She tugged until we heard the scratchy sound of ripping fabric. I saw the taffeta in her clamped fists, watched, silently, as Hetty tore the dress away from the zipper. She sat down on the floor, sobbing and hiccuping, in the middle of her honeymoon clothes. Startled by her fierce temper, I gasped. It had all come undone in one huge burst: the tightly guarded secrets of the Lodz ghetto and the hoity toity wedding in University City, who the Berkowitz family had been in Poland and who the Berks were trying to be now. Several blocks away, a siren screamed. I pulled Terry Sue right out of there.

April 3, 1963

Dearest Henrietta (she wrote to Hetty from the Missouri State Mental Hospital),
The more weeks and months I spend in this prison — oops, I mean hospital — the more time I have to think. Recently, I've started to wonder whether I might have once had a different life. Do you believe that is possible? One of the inmates here — her name is Velma — told me that she was a bear in her past life. She says that when she was a child, she had fleeting past life memories that she could use her paws and hind legs to climb trees. When she was four years old, she moved right out of her body and saw her bear self on a branch high up in a maple tree. Now she spends all of her free time, many hours every day, questioning all of us here about our past lives. Velma says that she is looking for clues to show that we were also once animals, too, like elephants, giraffes and rhinos. (Nobody here claimed to be a rhino.) Sometimes Velma writes poetry about past lives — hers and ours — and reads her poems to us. I think if I ever figure out anything about my past life, I'll draw what I was before I became Terry Sue Berk. You know, it's possible that I once lived as a penguin or as one of our great-great-grandmothers either on Mama's or Papa's side. I

don't know their first names, but on Papa's side, her last name would have been Berkowitz and on Mama's side she would have been Finklemann. Did I get that right? Velma told me that people sometimes avoid the subject of past lives due to violence in a previous lifetime. She also says that people could have lived in the body of the opposite sex. I don't think that's true. But, Hetty, do you think I was always a girl? Velma says that I could have been a boy in my past life and I don't know whether to believe her. (Maybe that's why I need pills to get my period.) Write soon and tell me if you think Velma knows what she's talking about. I'm not sure, but I like her poems. The best ones are about herself.

   Lots of love, Terry Sue

   T.S *Please don't repeat anything I wrote in this letter to anyone, not even to Lenny. If you do, I'll tell every doctor, nurse and janitor in the Missouri State Mental Hospital that your name Hetty is short for Henrietta and in your previous life, you were Henry!*

   More love, T.S.

   P.P.S. *Please don't forget to write me again soon.*
   More love, T.S

Nine

I DIDN'T SAY GOOD MORNING to Tilya the next day when I saw her at breakfast. We were alone in the kitchen. I was listening to the crackle of my Rice Krispies while she was reading a book. I didn't pump her for details about her date with Robby the night before even though I really did want to know. She looked up and poured some orange juice for me though I hadn't asked for any. Its yellowy colour turned my stomach. I didn't ask her if she knew how Mama was feeling two days before Hetty's wedding or what time Papa had left for work. I assumed that Terry Sue was still sleeping. The blinds throughout the house were shut to ward off the heat wave forecasted on the radio.

After a long silence, I said, "Why didn't you tell me about The Berkowitz Guide to Surviving in the Lodz Ghetto?"

She continued to read her book by Friedrich Engels, who, she'd informed me yesterday, was a friend of her favourite author Karl Marx.

"What are you talking about? I've never heard of The Berkowitz Guide to anything." A floor fan, pointing toward the table, moved from right to left, cooling our calves and ankles.

"You're lying." I poured my half finished bowl of cereal into the sink and washed the soggy Rice Krispies down the drain. "I know you must have heard about Papa's rules. You were in the Lodz ghetto with them."

Tilya placed the book by Engels on her lap. She swung her legs around to face me at the sink. "I'll tell you the exact reasons why that's impossible. It's a short list." From past arguments with her, I'd learned that Tilya's list making was sometimes the same as picking a fight. She raised her voice louder than the whirring of the floor fan and launched into the reasons for not knowing Papa's rules.

"To begin with," Tilya said. "I was born in October of 1940. I wasn't even alive when Mama, Papa and Hetty were forced into the ghetto. So how could I possibly have known about this Berkowitz Guide?" She sounded like we were on opposite sides in a court of law. "That's my first point."

"Secondly, I was a young child during the years we were sealed inside that ghetto." My eyebrows drifted toward the middle of my forehead. "How could I have understood the concept of rules or survival or barbed wire?"

I looked at the clean dishes in the dish drainer. I thought, might as well put them away. "Number three," Tilya continued, "we had no paper, no pencils, nothing to write with. How do you think father was going to make a book of rules?" I took a dishtowel to dry a clean tea cup before placing it in the cupboard. Tilya said, "Hetty cried a lot because she couldn't go to school. Even if there was a school for her to go to, she would have had nothing to write with. "

I said, "Okay, Tilya. You win." She didn't stop. "I also remember that father was very tired when he came home. There wasn't much to eat. You think he had the energy to make up rules?"

I fiddled with the radio sitting at the back of the counter. A station came in, faintly.

"Furthermore," Tilya said, "why are you so obsessed with Lodz and the ghetto anyway? Go call your friend Fruma. Ride your bike to the park before it gets too hot to play outside. And take Terry Sue with you."

"She's still sleeping," I said.

"Both of you should be happy that you can go outside. We never got to do that." She lifted the book by Engels off her lap and buried her face in it.

I put the milk back in the ice box and returned the cereal to the kitchen cabinet, stealing a glance at the title of the Engels book. "Well," I said, not prepared to back down. "Why are you so obsessed with your book on *The Condition of the Working Class in England*? Is that more interesting and important to you than the Lodz ghetto?"

"Did Hetty fill your head with this stuff about Papa's rules?"

I put a piece of rye bread into the toaster. The butter on the counter was at room temperature, soft and spreadable, just the way I liked it. I wanted to explain to Tilya, in case she hadn't read it in one of her great books, that rules could be important. Maybe The Berkowitz Guide to Surviving could help Terry Sue who needed to survive right now.

"Did you know that Hetty ripped her wedding dress last night?" I said.

Tilya shrugged as if weddings and marriage were not worth her time. I popped up the bread in the toaster before it turned medium brown and left the kitchen to call Fruma. I still believed that Papa must have written down the rules, no matter what Hetty or Tilya told me. I figured that the Guide was hidden somewhere in our house. Under a mattress or in a sock drawer. I dialled Fruma's number and tried to imagine staying inside all the time. It was possible that Papa's Rule #3 was: No playing games outside. I couldn't decide whether to wake Terry Sue or not.

Hetty surprised us at dinner by avoiding any discussion of her ripped wedding dress. Whatever way she intended to solve the problem, she kept it to herself. She had not slit her wrists, chopped off her hair, or thrown herself down the stairs. Maybe a good shopper always had an extra dress or two in the closet or knew where to get one, fast. Hetty's mood seemed to improve as the wedding day drew closer. She walked around the house almost as lightly as a pillow of lavender air. Her shoulders were less rounded, less heavy with sadness. At the dining room table, she began recalling mealtimes in the ghetto. We'd never talked about the food in Lodz before.

"Do you remember," Hetty said looking directly at Mama and Papa, "how we tried to guess what Polish people outside the Lodz ghetto were eating while we were starving inside?" I fidgeted in my chair, worried that mother would start to cry. I reminded myself that starving inside the ghetto and Terry Sue starving herself in front of us were two different things.

"Remember, we imagined they were eating hot barley soup with chocolate dumplings." Father tossed his head back and laughed, displaying the bulge in his throat, which was very large.

Tilya said, "And what about sauerkraut and whipping cream?"

"I knew you remembered things from Lodz," I hissed at Tilya. I decided to pester her about The Berkowitz Guide later. "Don't tell any more stories until I get back from the bathroom." I hated how often I had to pee and how much it burned when I did. Leaving the table, I saw Terry Sue tuck her boiled potato behind her back.

Papa asked Hetty and Tilya if they remembered a man named Rumkowski in the ghetto. "A big *macher*," Papa said.

"You mean a big shot," I called back to him.

"Well," Papa continued as I was leaving the dining room. "When Rumkowski stood on his soapbox to make a speech, he'd yell so loud and become so excited that he would wet his pants."

"What happened to this Rumkowski?" I said as soon as I returned to the table. None of them laughed.

"He was gassed to death," Mama said. She pushed her plate of cabbage rolls away. "In Auschwitz."

I glanced at Terry Sue's cabbage roll that was supposed to be comforting and hearty and sweet and sour and show how much Mama loved her. Terry Sue had not bothered to cut it into bite-size pieces because she wasn't going to take one bite whether Mama's cabbage rolls were intended to mean love or not.

I'd prefer to skip the subject of Hetty's wedding at Beth Israel. If I had a gigantic erasure, I'd wipe the whole thing away. The awkward gap between the Abrams and Berk families, the whispering and the staring, the fear Mama tucked into her mother-of-the-bride pillbox hat, Papa's blue hair, the wedding crasher, the sweltering heat. I'd like to forget all of it, starting with the large slabs of marble in the Beth Israel lobby, inscribed in gold lettering with the name of synagogue ex-presidents and past presidents, chairmen of committees and sub-committees, board members and non-board members going way, way back. A lot of them were named Abrams.

"They must be relatives of Lenny," I said to Tilya.

"So," she said.

"I'm just saying."

When we arrived at the shul, the photographer was arranging poses for a group shot of the Abrams family, placing each perfectly outfitted brother, sister, and grandchild in the correct position. Lenny waved at Hetty to join him in the center of the photo. She took his hand, as if she were Cinderella, in her wedding gown magically spun back together by our neighbourhood seamstress.

"Hetty looks like a princess in story book," Terry Sue said to me.

"You do, too." I lied to make her feel good. Her slender

body, clothed in a gauzy dress with capped sleeves and a tightly wrapped pink cummerbund, resembled an underfed ballerina. The capped sleeves were a big mistake. "Can I take your picture?"

My Brownie Hawkeye felt heavy dangling on my wrist. It was too big and boxy to fit in my purse and ridiculously out of place. I brought it so someone could take our picture and I would have my own photo of our family at the snazzy Beth Israel, one of the six of us before everything changed. Mama complained that she was too tired to have her picture taken and had to sit down. For fifteen minutes, she dozed in a folding chair. Papa didn't want his picture taken because he had tried to cover the gray in his hair the night before the wedding with some sort of rinse and now had jet blue streaks, like Veronica in *Archie* comics.

Right before the wedding procession was set to start, when we were waiting at the back of the sanctuary for the wedding party to assemble, I convinced Mama and Papa to stand on either side of Terry Sue for a photo. I told them to say cheese, but they didn't move their lips. They looked frozen, like ice sculptures at a winter carnival. But it was August and Hetty's wedding wasn't that sort of a fun-time event. Well, not until Robby showed up, breathless from running the two blocks from his house on Waterman to Beth Israel. When it was Ti-lya's turn to walk down the aisle, he insisted on joining her, waving to the guests on either side of the muted-colour carpet, tripping over his ratty sandals, making clown faces, being cute and shameless and odd and an atheist.

Hetty followed with Mama on her right and Papa on her left. Unsteady, they took timid steps along the runway that dipped and then crested as they reached the wedding canopy. Once or twice, their eyes turned upward. The arc of the ceiling soared above. Through the sky-high windows poured the late afternoon light. I didn't laugh or cry, but Terry Sue did both.

April 27, 1963

Dearest, sweetest baby sis (she wrote to me from the Missouri State Mental Hospital),
   This is a quick note to tell you about a book that I just finished reading. I think you might really like it. This is the first book I really enjoyed. Usually I don't have the energy to read. It's hard for me to even concentrate on reading the newspaper at night. But this is a really great book. I finished it in two days. Then I returned it to Hal who lent it to me in the first place. I've already forgotten the name of it. I've forgotten a lot of things. I'm going to dinner now, but I don't feel like eating much. Thank you for your recent letter to me, and I'll write again soon.
   Love you tons, Terry Sue

Ten

THE SUMMER BEFORE TILYA LEFT for New York in 1963, she changed her name to Toni. God help anyone that used her old name. Either she'd curse at you or give you the silent treatment for two whole days. Her undergraduate years at Washington University were well behind her. She'd been working at a shoe company for a year before continuing her studies. Graduate school at Columbia was now less than a week away. Father bought Toni a Smith Corona electric typewriter to take with her. It came with a black and a red typewriter ribbon. I inherited her upright manual Underwood, designed to sit on a desk and go nowhere. And it had a sticky "s" key.

At the start of the Labour Day weekend, Toni and Robby were flipping through their high school yearbook in the living room. I thought this must be one of those things people do when they know they are soon parting. From the kitchen, I overheard them reading the quips under the photos of their high school friends. Robby paused when he came to his own picture.

"Robertson George Sloan III." He raised his voice to ensure that the world could hear him. "We're all in the sewer, but some of us are bound for Dante's inferno." He laughed as if that quip were something to brag about. "It's kind of interesting to be evil, don't you think?"

I missed what Toni replied because I was dropping forks

and knives into the cutlery tray in the kitchen. I did, however, hear Robby tell Toni that his parents were going camping on Saturday and Sunday. They were leaving him in charge of the house, which included his younger brother and sister. I looked at mother to see if she was listening. I couldn't remember when she had last gone outside. She traipsed into the living room, passing before them in her nightgown a foot longer than her robe. I trailed two steps behind.

I said, "Do you want some lemonade, Robby?" I jingled the ice cubes in my glass. "I'll put extra ice cubes in for you."

As soon as mother disappeared up the stairs, I asked Robby if I could come to his party. I was supposed to have a sleepover at Fruma's on Saturday night, but I was prepared, just this once, to ditch her. I'd fake a stomach ache and turn gut wrenching ocher, then get better just in time to go to Robby's house. Fruma would never know, and her feelings couldn't possibly be hurt. A person had a right to be sick. That's what I'd tell her if she wanted to know what happened.

"Who said I'm going?" Toni said. "And even if I do go, you're not coming with me."

Robby said to Toni, "I don't mind. She can play with Gillian and Jake." I'd heard about them once before when Jake nearly blew up the Sloan basement. He was practicing a chemistry experiment for the school science fair. "They're cute kids, my little sister and brother." Robby scanned the middle part of my body while Toni turned the pages of her yearbook. He winked at me. "You'll like them."

"You are not going," Toni repeated. "Anyway, why would you want to?" Her question suggested that she was open to a strong argument. I didn't have one, at least not a reason I wanted to share with her.

"It's the last time you have to *schlep* me along with you," I said. On Saturday night, I stayed home in case she had changed her mind. As she approached me on the front porch, I couldn't tell if she was going to strangle or hug me. She muttered, "Let's go."

The houses on Waterman east of Big Bend Boulevard had big verandahs and wide front lawns. It was a quiet area where families had likely owned the same house for generations. Old trees lined the streets and trimmed hedges separated the properties, except for Robby's house that sat in the middle of the block and looked shabbier than the others. The paint on his verandah was peeling and the outer edge of the second step was splitting apart. Also, several of the spindles were attached to the railing with sort of thick tape. Squinting up at the roof, I became intrigued with a round window on the top floor. It resembled the window on a passenger ship, similar, I imagined, to a porthole on a boat that once sailed to America with the Berkowitz family on it. As we started to walk up the front path, a stray dog wandered by, his wiry reddish hair skimming my bare leg. Toni tried to kick him away, but she wasn't fast enough to prevent a light spray of something touching my leg.

"Yuck," I said. "Since when do dogs piss on people?" I wiped my leg with a Kleenex. The dog trotted into Robby's backyard like an invited guest.

Most of the other guests in Robby's backyard wore black T-shirts and baggy shorts. They seemed to be the usual poets, musicians, and artists drawn like magnets to the charismatic Robertson George Sloan III. Some I recognized from their pictures in the U. City High yearbook and others were unfamiliar to me. They were bunched together in the corner of the Sloan garden where a booth was located. I didn't know if it was a rain shelter, a fort, or a Christian version of a *Sukkah*. Toni and I joined them. I listened to their low, serious voices talking about subjects that seemed to really matter. One bearded guy mentioned that Andre Gide received a Nobel Prize before he died. Very important, I said to myself, although I was thinking about last night's challah with raisins. It was a special treat for Toni. Maybe her last challah.

"Why does Robby have a booth in his backyard?" I suspected, as soon as the words left my mouth, that I should never have asked Toni about the backyard booth. She ignored my question for a while. My legs were getting tired, especially the one that smelled like dog piss.

She said, "It's a gazebo."

That's when I knew Toni would leave us. She was going to New York and not coming back.

Inside the gazebo, candles floated in punch bowl filled with water. Robby sat on a high back chair at a card table draped in a white sheet, as if he were a priest or a prophet. I wanted to reach out and smooth his tousled, dirty blond hair, but he was busy cutting up a dead gerbil.

Someone shouted, "Hey, it's not Brill's tenth grade bio class, you know." Suddenly, ears and feet flew through the air. The tail almost hit me. Then he pulled a wadded strip of paper from a paper bag. Unfolding it, he looked for someone in the crowd.

"Julia, there you are," he said. "Here's what I predict will happen to you in the days to come. You will lose your virginity on your first night in New Haven, become pregnant, and be forced to drop out of the famed Yale School of Drama." Julia sucked in her stomach and tightened her cinch belt. "You'll spend the rest of your life making macaroni and cheese for your twelve children. You'll never act again." He shrugged his shoulders and dropped her fortune on the gazebo floor.

"More," someone shouted. Robby made circles with his arms. I guessed he was summoning spirits from somewhere.

"Okay, Craig." He smirked at him and pulled another fortune from the bag. "You will become a football coach at a state university. That's what you get for cheating on the Graduate Record Exams." He flung the strip of paper into the audience.

I told Toni that I needed to wash my leg in the bathroom. She turned to Julia who was frowning. I had no way of telling whether Julia had a naturally frowny face or was annoyed with what Robby said about her. Nobody else seemed to be concerned. Toni said to her, "Can you take my little sister to the bathroom?"

"Sure," Julia said. She led me to the back door of Robby Sloan's house. "The bathroom is on the second floor. Just walk through the kitchen and you'll find the front staircase."

Someone in the Sloan family loved to cook. I stood in their kitchen, impressed by the copper pots hanging over the gas stove and a spice rack filled with exotic dried herbs I'd never heard of or tasted. I wondered if Tilya now considered herself a spice maven with special knowledge of basil, marjoram, and thyme. Salt and pepper were as fancy as our family got. Whisks and tongs — never. Family photos snaked up the wall in frames that didn't match, grainy black and white pictures, one of a toddler squatting on a hiking trail, pooping. My eyes settled on a picture of Gillian splashing in a puddle. She wore Wellies and a raincoat that was just like mine. The only difference was that she had blonde hair and her grandparents were there.

Off the kitchen, there was a sunroom — a breakfast nook Toni called it when she sometimes slipped into their skin — with a maple table and piles of *National Geographic* magazines. A stack of sheet music rested on a stool. Gillian, I think, was the family musician. I wandered into the dining room where the piano was located, jumping back when I heard the purr of a cat tiptoeing along the keyboard. My nose began to twitch. More books were on the dining room table. Bookmarks were tucked into several of them. At the head of the table, one book propped open another. More books sat on the far side of the piano bench. I turned the pages of the leather bound book on top. All I saw were physics formulas.

My eyes were watering as I opened the double doors into the living room. On either side of the fireplace, tall bookcases were crammed with oversized books on art, architecture, and travel. A book with a coffee-stained jacket and a strange title rested on the rounded arm of the sofa. What an odd place, this Sloan house of books seemed to me. Our house didn't even have a bookshelf on the first floor. When I wanted to read, I walked to the U. City library on Delmar where the librarians all knew me. I was the dark-haired girl who renewed *The Diary of Ann Frank* every two weeks. I paused in the living room long enough to skim the first paragraph of *The Golden Bough*. I sneezed into the page by accident and quickly returned the book to the arm of the sofa. Not the book I was looking for.

In the front hallway, I groped for the banister leading to the second floor. A window with stained glass permitted a speck of light to shine on the first landing. The uncarpeted stairs creaked. Muffled voices came from the room to the right of the bathroom. I thought I heard groans and a bed squeaking as if someone was rocking up and down on it. Giggles came from the bedroom at the front of the house. Suddenly the door flew open. A naked guy staggered toward me on his way to the toilet.

"Oh, hi." I cleared my throat. "I was just...."

From behind, someone tapped my shoulder. "Where have you been?" Robby said. His faced softened, but not much. "We've been looking all over for you."

"I was just...."

"Well, while you're here, do you want to see my room?" He fumbled for something in the pocket of his shorts.

"I only wanted..."

He nodded his head toward the narrow staircase leading to the third floor. "My room is in the attic."

"Might as well, while I'm here," I nodded.

The first thing to catch my attention in Robby's room was his bed: a soiled mattress on the plank floor half covered by dandelion-patterned sheets. A guitar lay in the corner, a coffee-stained copy of *Ten Songs by Woody Guthrie* beside it. I sat down in his canvas director's chair, my knees pressed together, staring at the cigarette burns on the tangled sheets. Robby was stretched out on the bed, watching the flies swarming around the light overhead. He got up to switch it off. When he found me, he bent down to touch his face to mine. I felt his tongue, big, fleshy, wet and bitter, sloshing around in my mouth. I searched for the round window in his attic, the porthole on a passenger ship. I couldn't see much with the light turned off.

"Relax," he said. "I'm not going to hurt you." The sound of passing cars on Waterman seemed unreal. He stroked my hair. I strained to hear the noise coming from the second floor.

After a few minutes, I said, "I will, but ... it's so dark in here." He unzipped his shorts and rubbed something hard against me.

"So, it's dark in here," he said. He started to breathe quickly. His tongue was in my ear. He pressed his face into my neck and kissed me. I felt his arms clasping me to him, his chest rolling over my breasts.

"Well," I stammered. "Okay, but...." He stroked my hair again.

"But what?" He fumbled with the bottom three buttons of my blouse. I couldn't say anything. The ability to speak was beginning to drown inside of me.

I took a big breath in. "Well," I said again. His smoky smell repulsed me. "You know, your mother."

"Yeah." He kissed my other ear. "I know my mother. What about her?" He laughed softly, as if he was remembering something funny from another time.

"Well," I said. "She knows about genetics, right?" He rubbed himself against my stomach.

"She's a geneticist, yeah." He was panting, squishing against me. "So what?"

"Well," I said, turning my head toward the window.

"Do we have to talk about this now?" he murmured. Something sticky landed on my stomach.

"Well," I said. "Do you have any of her books around here?" I pulled my blouse over my stomach to wipe off the wetness.

He burst into laughter.

"Don't laugh," I said. I wiggled my legs away from his thighs.

"You're a crazy kid, you know that," he said.

"No, I'm not."

"I think you are. That's why I like you."

I tried to push him away. "Well, I just want to borrow one of your mother's books."

"Why would you want to do that?" He grabbed my wrists and pinned them over my head.

"Well..." I felt trapped, like being handcuffed.

"Well what?" He kissed my nipple through my half-buttoned blouse.

"Maybe one of her books would explain something."

"Like what?"

"Like why my sister isn't eating and how maybe it has something to do with what was passed down to her." I squirmed out of his grip, feeling the sting of tears running down my face. "That's what the encyclopedia said genetics is about. What's so crazy about that?" I brushed his saliva off my neck with the palm of my hand. On the way to the door, I stumbled over some paperbacks on the floor.

"Watch out," Robby said. "I dropped my mother's genetics textbook somewhere around there." His laugh followed me down the stairs.

August 1, 1963

Dear esteemed second sister (she wrote to Toni from the Missouri State Mental Hospita),
You don't know how happy it made me to hear from you. I'm very pleased that you won a scholarship to Columbia for graduate school. It offers great opportunities for your advancement and for meeting a nice young man. (Hint. Hint.)

My new doctor, Dr. Gillman, has been very kind to encourage me to draw and attend recreational therapy. There's not much happening here, but basket weaving is better than doing nothing. I doubt that Mama told you that we met with Dr. Gillman a few days ago. She's always so secretive about me. Of all my doctors, he is the only one I felt wasn't lying to us. He told Mama, Papa and me that it looks like I can't have children. I'm turning seventeen soon and, by this time, my ovaries should have been producing certain kinds of hormones that make it possible for married girls to have babies. He said that my ovaries failed to function like that. I thought Mama would plotz in his office. Then she said, right in front of Dr. Gillman who hardly knows our family, that first she lost her sister Tzophie, her precious niece Shana, and her handsome nephew Yitzy. Yitzy, she told Dr. Gillman, could have been a movie star. That's how handsome he was. Now she was losing some of her future grandchildren and her great grandchildren because I'll never have babies.

I feel so terrible for Mama and Papa. I'm just not sure how much they really want to know about me. Knowing Mama, I can only think that she is trying to protect us from something she fears will hurt us, all of us. You know how superstitious she is.

Tons of love, Terry Sue

P.S. You are the only person in the family that I can write this to and don't tell anyone else. I thought you might understand the problem with my genes and ovaries. Also, you might meet a nice young doctor at Columbia who can make my ovaries work. Then I won't need to feel so guilty about my one lonely little X chromosome that never had another X to be its mate. Maybe if I had known about this sooner, I could have done something about it, like eating the right food or walking more. Too late now.

Love again, T.S.

P.P.S. Actually, I like your real name Tilya better than Toni, but if you feel that Toni will help you meet a nice young doctor sooner rather than later, then I'm all for it. When you find him, could you please ask him to check my medical records as soon as possible. I'd really appreciate it. I've never seen one word that the doctors and nurses have been written about me.

Love again and again, T.S.

P.P.P.S. Wouldn't it be funny if I changed my name from Terry Sue to Terrence? I could be your brother instead of your sister. I know that would make Mama and Papa very happy because we all know that they wanted at least one boy in the family. And a name change might also solve the missing chromosome problem.

Love you forever and a day, Terrence (I hope you like my new name) Berk

Eleven

I WAS THE ONLY OTHER PERSON in the house when she screamed. From her bedroom, Mama let out a wail — a *geshrie* Papa called her panicked shrieks — so terrible that I thought she had seen an alien or a mouse. I finished putting on my tights and scoop neck leotard for the modern dance rehearsal at school. Before heading downstairs, I peeked into her room.

"You don't look great, Mama." I didn't have time for the details. Mr. Kettlecreek had warned me twice about being late for home room class. A third warning came with a suspension.

"Can I get you a glass of water before I leave?" I took a few steps toward her. The room was chaotic, as if the walls were vibrating from a tremor in the earth. Near her bed, I smelled her sweat-matted hair on the pillow.

"I don't feel so good." Her voice trembled. I looked away. No child should see a mother with her nightgown twisted around her waist. "My stomach is upside down," she said.

"Maybe you ate something that was spoiled before you went to bed." I covered her with a cotton blanket. She was still cooking for six, although I was the only kid at home. Potato kugel and boiled chicken sat in the back of the ice box from one Shabbat to the next, or one holiday to the next, whichever came first.

"No, no. It's not something bad that I ate. I had a dream about your sister," she said.

"Which sister? I have three, you know." She didn't seem to understand that I was in a hurry so I held up my watch for her to see. I missed my sisters. Not because they were no longer here. Even if they were all standing by Mama's bed this moment, something would still be missing. I couldn't imagine caring for anyone more than I cared for them, but it didn't feel like we were the same family. Every time I thought of Toni, I felt strange. I wasn't sure that she knew about Robby and me. I tapped my finger on my watch. "I'm going to be late."

"Something happened when they moved Terry Sue back to Barnes Hospital yesterday. Something awful, like in my dream," Mama said.

"Your pills, Mama. Where are they? I'm going to miss my home room class?" Her eyelids sagged. Little white bumps dotted the lines under her eyes. Maybe the mind isn't a beautiful thing. That's what I thought looking at her face.

"In my dream, Terry Sue turned into a peach."

For a moment I tried to imagine what a peach girl would look like. She'd have a bloated stomach with toothpick skinny legs, a soft fuzzy face and a pug nose, nothing too scary.

"So, what's so horrible about a peach?" I said.

"But something happened to her when she got to be a peach," Mama said. "She was in the Lodz forest and she fell off the branch of a tree. She was rolling on the ground, crying for help. A *boychick* taking an afternoon walk found her. He bent down to touch her face and took a bite of my Terry Sue."

"You'll have to tell me the rest later or tell Papa when he gets home from work." I retreated to the door of her room. "Besides, Terry Sue was never in Lodz."

"The *boychik's* teeth, you should know before you go to school, crunched down on something hard. He bit into her and then spit the fruit into the palm of his hand."

"I have to go or Mr. Kettlecreek will hit the ceiling."

"So he sends you to the principal's office. *Nu?*" She continued. "The *boychick* saw a twisted bone inside the peach, like a toe. Then one of her ears, all crooked, fell from a hole at the top of the peach. Then a thumb without a nail, and a shrivelled, a shrivelled you-know-what, and a thick *gebroken* neck. He took one look at the parts of my Terry Sue and he threw the twisted, broken pieces of the peach as far as he could throw them through the forest. When he finished, he sat down by the tree and ate her sweet flesh."

She closed her eyes and tossed from side to side in bed. The cotton blanket became twisted around her waist again. Weekend newspapers crumpled underneath her hips. She rolled over to reach for the pills on her night table, stretching her arm as far as it would go. A pink sheet of paper, creased into thirds, lay partly under her on the bed. It seemed to be the same stationary that Terry Sue used to write to us.

"Mama, what are you sleeping on?" I said. "It's always such a mess in here." I started to tidy up around her.

"Tilya," she said.

I hated how she confused us, or worse, how she often scrolled through all of our names, in one breath, before she got to mine. I didn't remind her of Tilya's name change.

"Tilya was in the dream," she said. I glanced at my watch. One thing I never doubted about mother: whatever she concocted in her head made sense if you listened in a certain way. I decided to skip home room rather than arrive late.

"Would you like breakfast?" I said, famished after she described the sweet flesh of the peach in her dream. I helped her out of bed and guided her down the steps to the kitchen, leaving all the accumulated stuff on her bed. In the ice box I found a jar of kosher dills, two eggs, pistachio halvah from Hanukah last year and some limp celery.

"I think I'll throw away these pickles," I said as I looked for something to eat. They were floating in mouldy brine. "They've seen better days."

"We hid Tilya in an old pickle cellar," she said. "You should know before you go to school, she slept in a crate sitting on the shelf." I wrote a note to Mr. Kettlecreek explaining why I missed home room and first period math class, but omitted the part about mother's peach dream and Tilya sleeping in a damp hole in the ground where pickles were stored. He'd probably think I was lying.

The leotard layered under my flared skirt and wool sweater felt clingy. It was the third and last lunch period of the day. Fruma and I were eating lunch in our normal spot —a corner near the window at the far end of the cafeteria. Several trays had been abandoned near us, littering the table with banana peels and milk cartons. Stragglers snapped the latches on their lunchboxes, their used forks clunking on the linoleum. The overheated air likely contributed to the prickly feeling of my sweater. My legs were crossed. I lifted half the cupcake Fruma gave me to my mouth, grateful for it because I hadn't eaten at home. She talked about the algebra test that I had missed in the morning. Fruma was positive that she had flunked the test, even though she was a genius and excelled in everything. She was unscrewing the top on her thermos just as an announcement came from the PA system.

"Attention all students. Will Linda Sue Berk please report directly to the principal's office." I recognized the voice of the principal, Mr. Boytner, also known as Mr. Boyish-Goyish.

I said to Fruma, "Don't move." A tortoiseshell headband kept the hair off her forehead. "Boyish-Goyish is going to tell me something terrible happened. I just know it."

"Don't be silly," she said. "Besides, why do you always think the worst?" I stopped breathing though my legs continued to knock together, like high-speed egg beaters. "You know what your problem is?" Fruma said. "There's always some catastrophe waiting for you. And most of the time your fears don't make any sense."

The only sound in the cafeteria came from quick feet scuffling toward the double doors. I wanted to follow those feet to a stall in the girls' bathroom where I could hide or run away through the back exit. The fear of Mr. Boyish-Goyish, what he might say, turned my *kishkas* inside out, but there was no point telling Fruma that.

"How much can kids growing up in U. City know about real catastrophes anyway?" Her flat tone suggested that I shouldn't bother to answer. She dumped the core of her apple and thermos into her lunch box.

"Nothing," I said anyway. "And everything."

When Mr. Boyish-Goyish made a second announcement, Fruma grabbed my arm and yanked me from the cafeteria to the principal's office. He greeted us in the hall, a lanky middle-aged man wearing a respectable suit and striped tie, his arms folded over his chest, his crew cut standing at solemn attention. He ushered me into his office and wiped a few tears from his eyes. I'm not sure he wanted me to see him crying so I acted like I hadn't noticed.

"Linda Sue, you need to go home."

Fruma and I didn't hurry. We walked up and down blocks with no plan and, for once, not jabbering either. When we crossed Hanley Road at Cornell Avenue, she said, "You know, you'd feel a lot better if you would stop being so stubborn and just cry for her." It occurred to me that Fruma could have failed her algebra test in first period this morning. Hard to believe, but she might not be as smart as I thought she was.

"It could be a tear duct problem." I said.

Fruma said, "Who knew you're an eye specialist all of a sudden?" It was early November, and the wind was so strong that it nearly blew us down the hill. An eyelash from my eye became lodged on my eyeball. I pinched the skin of my eyelid with my fingers and popped it in and out until the eyelash disappeared. My eyes teared a little, maybe because something was still in there. Or it could have been tears from the dream Mama told me about a sweet tasting peach that fell from a tree.

November 2, 1963

Dearly beloved little sis (she wrote to me from Barnes Hospital),
   This might be the last letter I can send you. Sorry for the wobbly writing, but my fingers are getting too weak to hold the pen. I think I was moved back to Barnes Hospital because my kidneys are failing, but I'm not sure because nobody ever explains anything to me.
   Did Toni ever tell you that I can't have children? I asked her not to say anything to you, but I have a hunch that nothing I say in my letters is kept private. Anyway, in case Toni didn't spill the beans, Mama, Papa, and I had a meeting with Dr. Gillman. I didn't think you'd understand so I decided not to mention it to you. He said my ovaries don't work. Well, that's not exactly what he said. He used words like defective genital development. You probably don't know what ovaries or defective genital development mean. I know I didn't before Dr. G. said that my ovaries are useless. Well, what he meant was that my ovaries are not capable of making a healthy egg that can become fertilized and form an embryo. It's all pretty complicated although I don't see why I can't just borrow someone's healthy eggs to make babies. There must be somebody who has more eggs than she needs. I'll ask Cuddles (he still comes often to play monopoly with me) to look into it because if I'm ever able to have a baby, I'd want it to be with him. I don't know if Mama and Papa would

approve. He may not be Jewish. I'll have to ask him his last name and let you know.

Anyway, I just wanted to tell you not to worry about me. I'm in a safe place. I love our family and I know you'll keep me in your heart forever. Oh, did I thank you for all the letters you have written to me? I re-read them often.

Yours forever, Terry Sue

P.S. I'm just wondering if you were ever able to figure out that drawing Dr. Richardson made for me a while ago, the drawing showing the pair of 46,XX chromosomes that normal girls have. I think I sent it to you or maybe I sent it to Toni when she was still Tilya. You probably burned it so no one will ever find out that I'm not normal. Dr. Richardson said that girls with 45,X makeup, like mine, are abnormal. I thought Mama would die on the spot when she heard that. I remember Dr. Richardson trying to reassure her by telling her that it was just a little mistake of nature that he could fix. I still don't understand what all the fuss is about. Either does Cuddles, if you know what I mean.

Love again, T.S.

Twelve

I DIDN'T CRY. Not at the chapel. Not during the eulogy. Not as she was lowered into the ground.

Not even when mourners began to shovel dirt onto her coffin, first father, then Uncle Herman followed by Lenny, Chaim Rubenstein, and others I didn't know. Just three spades full, thrown in by each of them. One by one, they dug the pointy end of the shovel into the earth and stepped aside, as if to put a period at the end of a life sentence.

"It's a *mitzvah* to fill in the grave with dirt. I mean a really, really pure good deed," Hetty whispered to me. She was wearing sunglasses though it was an overcast day in November. November 4, 1963, to be precise. Hetty did not believe children should attend funerals. Mourning was reserved for adults unless the dead person happened to be your sister. So I didn't understand why Toni had not come back from New York to be here.

A basin of water sat on our front porch when we returned from the grave. "Wash your hands," Hetty said. "To get rid of any demons that may have followed us home." She rubbed her finger tips dry with a nubby towel and passed it to me.

"What demons? I didn't see spooks hanging around Terry Sue's coffin unless you mean that hunched man who couldn't stop wiping his nose with the back of his hand during the eulogy."

"That man was Lenny's uncle Joe Abrams who, at least, was crying," Hetty said.

Inside, the house felt airless, like it was haunted by ghosts. That's how I viewed the sheets covering all the mirrors, anyway. They were the ghosts of dead people from a different time and place — Aunt Tzophie, Uncle Shmul, cousins Shana and Yitzy.

"*Tui, tui, tui,*" Hetty said when I told her my theory. "But don't peek under those sheets or the Angel of Death might grab you, too." To make myself less conspicuous to the angel, I avoided the stumpy chairs in the living room set up only for the immediate family, our family — what was left of it — stricken by grief that never seemed to end. "And don't wash your hair for the whole seven days," she said.

I rolled my eyes in the direction of the ceiling and tried to remember if Hetty was always this bossy. Ignoring her warnings, I approached the mirror in the hall, ready to lift a corner of the sheet. A chill seemed to rise from the edges of the covered glass. I felt invisible, as if I had died with my third sister.

As soon as Mama walked into the house, she went straight into the dining room, where she glanced at the trays of food that Mr. and Mrs. Abrams sent us. She climbed the stairs to her bedroom, undressed and put on the same nightgown she was wearing when she had the peach dream, getting up only to go to the bathroom. Papa tried to coax her to come downstairs, but she wanted to be alone. He brought her chicken soup and a Kaiser roll. She ate nothing. Sometimes I imagined mother's sadness seeping through her flesh onto the worn Persian carpet underneath the bed, spreading, like a spray of salty tears, across the room.

By early evening, family and friends started to gather at our house for the prayer service. We were waiting for more people to arrive when I asked Hetty to let me see one of the prayer books Rabbi Blumberg had brought with him. I wanted to be prepared for the Mourner's Kaddish, to be able to do a good job for Terry Sue.

"Forget it," she said. "Kaddish can only be recited in the presence of a minyan, which consists of ten adult Jewish men." She lowered her voice and pulled her sweater around her shoulders. I fought the urge to ask if I could read the verses in the prayer book without reciting them during the service. She wasn't letting me anywhere near those books.

Just before Rabbi Blumberg began, a few more people, mostly women, came through the door. "What if ten men don't show up? Then do I count?" I said.

"Then we go into the street hunting for them." I thought she was joking. Strangers from the street could say Kaddish for my sister and I couldn't. Hetty was teasing me, for sure.

"What about half men? Do they count?" I said, watching the prayer books circulate among the chosen.

She said, "What's that supposed to mean?"

I waited a moment. "Like people who are half men and half ladies."

"Don't be an idiot." She shooed me into the kitchen with the other women where we huddled together for almost half an hour, the drone of Rabbi Blumberg's voice broken up now and then by the sound of men mumbling in Hebrew very fast. For some reason, Hetty didn't seem to mind being shunted into such a small space reserved for women. A few relatives stayed after the service was over, including Joe Abrams who, I noticed, was carrying a handkerchief with him. I heard several people talking as I went upstairs.

"So how did she die?"

"A heart attack."

"She weighed only seventy-six pounds."

"Seventeen years old. A real tragedy."

I closed the door to my room, glad to be away from adult talk, and fell asleep immediately. When I woke up in the morning, Papa was sitting at the foot of my bed. Before I uttered a word about my exclusion from Kaddish, he told me that I wouldn't have been praying directly for her anyway.

"There's not one mention of death or the person who died in the entire prayer," he said.

I thought this over for a time. "I guess so." I had no way of knowing if father was right or wrong. "But do you think I can call Toni in New York?" I asked him. I hoped that she could explain Kaddish to me because she was studying the history of ideas at Columbia. So, whose great idea, I wanted to ask her, was it to banish women from prayers for a sister? And I needed to hear her voice, to know that she was still interested in something, anything, connected to us. I also wondered if she had heard from Robby recently. I promised to get a part-time job after school to pay back father for the long distance call. I swore that I would not make Toni feel guilty for missing Terry Sue's funeral. But honestly, I doubted whether she could possibly understand our complicated grief. How could she know when she was so far away?

On the last day of *shiva*, I slipped out of the house and headed for the playground at Jackson Park, hoping that I wouldn't see anyone I knew. My hair looked like a mass of frizzy tufts — my fault for listening to Hetty and not washing it for a week. Rocking back and forth on the swing, I felt the seat sinking lower and lower. I dug the toe of my penny loafer into the sandy ground and stared at it.

I remembered father once saying that I was named after his mother. Her name was Shaindel, my Hebrew middle name. That's why I'm Linda Sue in English. The "Sue" is for Shaindel, the same as it was for Terry Sue. Father always told us that his mother Shaindel had the heart of an angel. She'd share whatever food they had with the poor people of Lodz. Before they went into the ghetto, it must have been. I was so honoured to have my grandmother's name. But I had to admit, I didn't feel angelic now. I felt like a murderer. Terry Sue didn't need to die in the way that she did. I was the sister closest to her in age, the one who was paired with her most often. We had twin middle names and twin scars on our upper arms. Which made me, more than anyone, responsible.

After a few minutes, I started to drag my foot back and forth in the ground, making a smooth path with the side of my shoe. I bent over and picked up a handful of sand, watched the grains sift through my fingers. When I returned home, Mama was taking the ghost sheets off the mirrors. I listened to her shallow breaths. Her hands tugged at the white *schmattas* as if they had turned to stone. Growing up in the shadow of her grief had taught me next to nothing about the right way to grieve. Maybe there wasn't a right way. What if it went on forever?

Several days later, when the formal time of mourning was behind us, Papa went to The Mental to pick up a box containing the belongings of Terry Sue. The night he came home with the box was a chilly, but clear evening full of promise, the kind of night for a bike ride after dinner. In earlier years, Terry Sue and I might have cycled to Jackson Park, then stopped for grape popsicles at the corner drug store. (Popsicles never made it onto her list of forbidden foods.) Papa brought the box into the house, a medium-sized cardboard box no different from the ones stacked at the front of the supermarket. It was sealed with tape and her name was printed across the top of it. He put the box down on the line of tiles separating the foyer from the central hallway where it sat, untouched, for weeks. The box quickly became a piece of furniture. Instead of hanging my jacket in the closet, I dropped it conveniently on the box. Papa, I noticed, tried to avoid the box. He began using our back door more often. We had never been back door people before. He'd comment that the garbage was leaking or his shoes were muddy. All of a sudden, the back door was the best, the most efficient and expedient, the safest and the cleanest way, to exit and enter our house. Mama rarely left the house so the box in the foyer didn't seem to concern her. I wondered if she had even realized it was there. On Thursday after school, Fruma visited me, unexpectedly, to borrow *Death of a Salesman* for an English assignment. I ran up the stairs to get the play for her while she waited just inside the front door.

"What's in that box?" she asked when I returned. She had likely figured out it was a box related to Terry Sue because my jacket only covered the "Sue" in my sister's name. I studied Fruma's face, worried that she might have recently developed extrasensory perception. Her intuition might be telling her that a secret about Terry Sue lay hidden in the box.

I sat down on top of my jacket. "I'm not sure."

"Well, aren't you at least going to open it?" She shoved Arthur Miller's play into her knapsack with such force that her headband fell forward, landing on the bridge of her nose. She pushed the headband back with one hand and twisted the door handle with the other. "Well, thanks for this." I thought I detected horror in her gaze.

As soon as she was at the curb, I carried the box up the stairs, hugging it awkwardly in the crook of my elbows. I rested it on my knee several times before reaching the top.

Was I a snoop or a good sister? I felt guilty opening Terry Sue's box without some sort of permission and negligent if I didn't. What's worse, I asked myself. Neither Hetty nor Toni was around to advise me. They felt so far removed from our family that I couldn't imagine them caring whether I opened the box or not. I doubted if either one would argue over Terry Sue's possessions. What value would anything kept at The

Mental have anyway? A flannel nightgown or some cheap bracelets from the dimestore. Stuff like that. It seemed better to claim whatever was left of her than to ignore her small remains: one box.

I crouched over the box, knees bent, ready to use all my strength to push it into the middle of my room. My arms felt like dead weights, the opposite of oars gliding across a lake. Terry Sue had been gone, away from us, for a long time; yet I didn't miss her, really feel her goneness, until I was stooped over that corrugated box typically filled with a carton of milk, a loaf of Wonder bread and some luncheon meats. I took a letter opener from my desk, stabbed the tape holding the flaps of the box together, and pried open the top. My knees cracked as I squatted lower to the ground, which reminded me of something my Russian ballet teacher once told me when I tried to do a front split. He'd said: "The splits, my child, are like everything else in life." I had continued to scissor my straightened legs, forcing them closer and closer to the floor. He'd smiled and patted my head. "Only when you are ready and only if you really want to." Unpacking Terry Sue's box, I felt defeated and alone. Another part of me was disappointed that I would never be the great Russian dancer, Anna Pavlova, or play the part of a dying swan.

Framed photos were the first items I saw in the box. She had kept them on her dresser at The Mental. I recognized the blow-up of the picture I had taken of Terry Sue, Mama and Papa on the day Hetty got married. Whatever happened to my Brownie Hawkeye, I wondered. I think Kodak stopped making that model several years ago. The three of them looked so worn out. It must have been the camera or the lighting inside Beth Israel. Another photo in the box I didn't remember at all. It was of us, the four Berk sisters at Aunt Mimi's shack on the Meramec. I couldn't recall which summer it was taken or when we wore the straps of our bathing suits like that: half on, half off with too much of our chests showing. The professional photograph of Terry Sue, taken at Ashen-Brenner's Photography Studio, I knew very well. I went with Hetty and Terry Sue on that Saturday, downtown by bus, for the sitting. Hetty insisted that Terry Sue wear her frilliest party dress, the one which had a wide neckline and puffed sleeves with pleated elastic bands. She rarely wore the dress because she almost never got invited to parties.

Under the framed photos, I found a few of Terry Sue's crafts in the box. She had a flare for colouring flowers in shades of purple. The good luck charm we had purchased on the Admiral was in there, too. But I saw none of her clothes. Papa must have given them away or left them at The Mental for some other patient or inmate, as Terry Sue called the lifers. The thought of my sister spending decades locked up in The Mental was more than I could bear. Forgive me for asking, I wanted to say to every pediatrician, psychiatrist, and specialist that ever observed or treated or laid one medical finger on her, but what was so wrong with the way she was? That is, before she stopped eating and turned into a living cadaver. I couldn't stand to rummage through the box one moment longer. In fact, I couldn't stand to be in my room with the opened box anymore. If Fruma asked whether I had unpacked yet — and I knew she would question me in first period tomorrow — I could say yes without crossing my fingers or toes. She didn't need to know that the flaps on the box were taped shut again.

Less than a week later, I returned to the box. At the bottom were letters, some tucked into envelopes and others, loose pages in no particular order. I spotted my rainbow stationary in the pile, with my messy scrawl, which Terry Sue likely couldn't decipher. Several letters were signed "Hugs and kisses from Cuddles." Those went into the trash. Even touching them gave me the creeps. Hetty's letters to Terry Sue were the only the only ones that I read. She corresponded the most regularly with Terry Sue, always on white stationery with roses streaming down the left side of the page. I remembered the day she bought that stationary at Famous Barr for a reduced price. The roses, pictured in full bloom and printed on crisp paper, appeared hopeful. That's how we felt, back then, before she died. I saw no harm in reading Hetty's letters to Terry Sue. What difference did it make now? I had already pilfered Toni and Hetty's drawers in search of Terry Sue's letters to them. I'd found eleven of them and without telling Hetty or Toni, I had taken the letters into my room and read each one seven times. (I've included all of Terry Sue's letter to us in this short account of her life in the Berk family.)

I rifled through the box looking for a card, a note, a line from Mama and Papa to Terry Sue. I found nothing. Just as well because whatever they wrote would have probably been in Yiddish or Polish. I'd have to find a translator, someone who didn't live in University City, to read it to me. I couldn't ask the rabbi or my Sunday school teachers. What if Mama and Papa said things that they didn't want anyone else to know? There was nothing written in Yiddish or Polish in the box. Terry Sue must have destroyed Mama and Papa's letters to her so that nobody at The Mental would ever read them or know her secret.

The letters that Hetty had written to Terry Sue, during the years she was away, focused mainly on Hetty Abrams, wife and mother. In one letter, she told Terry Sue about the birth of her daughter Stacey — another blessed Shaindel in the family, she penned. One undated letter caught my attention.

Dearest, adored third sister (Hetty wrote to Terry Sue),
I hope you are doing well. We are all fine, though Joseph

and Stacey are keeping us very busy. I've been trying to teach them to swim with no luck. Lenny says we should put them in swimming classes, but I'd worry that the instructor might turn her head and they would drown. You know that children can drown in shallow water as easily as they can drown in deep water. I read in The Reader's Digest that children can drown in toilets, pails, and buckets of water used for cleaning around the house. I'm going to get Lenny to turn on the sprinkler for Joseph and Stacey to cool off instead of going to the pool at Heman Park. All of the public pools are so dirty and crowded in the summer. And it's polio season.

I was looking through some old paper recently, and I found something that I want you to have. It's a drawing that I had completely forgotten about. I made it when we were living in the Lodz ghetto. Tilya and I didn't have any toys to play with, no books or crayons and tablets. But one day Papa came home with a small scrap of paper that he found on the street and a piece of coal. He said that I should draw a funny picture to make Tilya laugh. She was just a little kid then, about the same age as my Joseph. So I thought and thought about what would amuse her. Before I knew it, I had drawn a cat sitting up on its hind legs with its paws curled up in front of its fury chest. The cat, as you can see in my drawing (sorry it's sort of smudged after so many years) has pointy ears and a big smile on its face. Tilya kept asking me why the cat was smiling. I had to make up something very quickly. I picked up the piece of coal and drew a cape and cloche hat on the cat. I told Tilya that the cat was happy because she was all dressed up for her best friend's birthday party.

I hope you like this little drawing as much as Tilya did. She always asked me to tell her stories about the dressed up cat. We'd spend hours in bed planning what the cat would wear to her next party, maybe a little black dress and nylon stockings *or a pert hat. The drawing is the only thing I have left from the terrible time that we almost didn't survive. I want you to have it. Hold onto this bit of paper, place it under your blanket where it will be safe, and remember every time you touch it that we love you. Don't give up. Eat whatever they put in front of you even if the food is vomitious and has pork in it. Just eat it anyway. Get fat like this dressed up cat so you can come home to us and pur-r-r-r!*

Hugs and kisses.
Hetty

Thirteen

I DREADED THANKSGIVING the year my sister died. To be honest, I dreaded Thanksgiving, period. For the last few years, we had gone to The Mental on Thanksgiving to visit Terry Sue and returned home to a quiet house. Mama and Papa didn't do Thanksgiving. Even when their rabbi told them that Jews were permitted by Jewish law to celebrate it — as long as the turkey was kosher — our parents were sceptical. Not that they weren't thankful to be here after what happened in Lodz. They were. Still, they preferred a roasted whole chicken, stuffed if we were lucky. For us, the fourth Thursday in November was just another Thursday, with slightly more food. Except for this year, which happened to be the first time Toni invited me to spend the weekend with her in New York.

When Toni had first proposed a Thanksgiving visit, I couldn't imagine what we would talk about for four days. Our long distance phone calls were usually distant and not long. How you doing? Fine. Studying hard? Very. When are you coming back to St. Louis? Never. I decided to go to New York anyway, undeterred by the prospect of one-word sentences and plenty of blanks in between. Besides, she might feel different about me when she saw how much I'd shot up recently, her height now, and no longer a kid. I was fifteen years old.

Mama, who couldn't have cared less about pilgrims landing on some rock in the middle of nowhere three centuries years ago, suddenly became adamant that I stay home for Thanksgiving. "You want a turkey?" she said. "I'll make you a beautiful bird."

Hetty grabbed the chance to have an American Thanksgiving. She bought me a ticket to New York for Wednesday night in the week before the holiday so that I'd be home in time for Mama's first real American Thanksgiving dinner. Papa drove me to the airport. "Do you need some money?" he said, kissing me goodbye. I shook my head. "Just don't forget to come back."

Toni lived in a cavernous apartment on Riverside Drive near Columbia, far too spacious for one person. Her roommate had dropped out of graduate school to get married in Georgia, taking everything, including her trundle bed, with her. I slept on an air mattress in the vacated bedroom. There were two ground rules, Toni said. Stay out of the kitchen late at night to avoid frolicking cockroaches and wipe your bum with caution. A hot water pipe, extending from floor to ceiling, stood next to the toilette. On Thursday I attended a seminar with her at Columbia; on Friday, we walked most of the way from Toni's apartment to the Metropolitan Museum of Art. In the mid-morning light, cold and brash, I noticed circles under her eyes.

On the steps to the museum, Toni said, "Remember Robby Sloan?" The Columbia University sweatshirt that I was wearing under my coat felt like one layer too many. I still hadn't revealed my encounter with Robby to her, not one sordid millisecond of it. "He's meeting us in the early afternoon, possibly for lunch." It didn't sound like he had disclosed the details to her either.

"What's he doing in New York? I thought he was at Yale studying theatre."

Toni guided me through the wooden vestibule into the Great Hall of the museum. "He is, but this weekend he's in the city. I thought you'd want to see him."

"Why didn't you tell me Robby was meeting us today?"

"You always liked Robby."

Toni opted for the medieval galleries to be our first stop. She didn't say why. The maze of rooms overwhelmed me, but not her. She knew the museum's floor plan without consulting a map and was able to navigate our way to the tapestries, church statues, and elaborately carved ivory boxes without a misstep. "Those are reliquaries," she said as we peered into one of the glass cases. Her hips tilted into mine. In the months since Terry Sue's death, I felt lost without her. "They're containers for sacred relics, like the bones of saints." I hadn't forgiven Toni for missing the funeral, and I wanted to tell her that. She glanced at her watch. "Time to go." We hurried through the medieval sculpture hall. "You'll have to come back to see the museum's Christmas tree some day. They mount it right here." We climbed the monumental staircase to the second floor for our rendezvous with Robby. I couldn't explain why, but I felt like we were stepping into history.

Robby arrived, scruffy, smelling of old cigarettes and unacceptably late. It was nearly two o'clock. I announced, as soon as I felt his eyes touch me, that I was going back to the medieval galleries. "Get thee to a nunnery," he said, waving me away with a dismissive flair. My face turned a splotchy, baby-girl pink.

"Wait," said Toni. "He's just teasing you. That's from Shakespeare, silly." She gave Robby a poke in the ribs. He tittered. Then both of them burst into uncontrollable giggles, doubling over in hysterics, as if they were now laughing about a different something.

"No, really, wait," he said as I was turning away from them. "I wanted to tell you both about this conference my mother went to several months ago."

"Why would you tell us about your mother's conference?" Toni said.

"Well, she thought you would be interested."

"Us, interested in your mother's conference?" she said with dwindling patience for Robby's theatrics.

"She remembered that I knew you."

"So you know us. Big deal." Toni said. I stood still, awed by the museum's architecture, the arches, each curve perfectly executed.

"And your sister Terry Sue," he said.

"What about her?" Toni said.

The conference that Robby proceeded to describe was held in Baltimore. The topic this year was fascinating, his mother had reported to him. A multidisciplinary panel, consisting of a geneticist, an endocrinologist and an ethicist, had been organized to consider a particular case — a famous case — a case that had occupied the attention of the medical community in St Louis for years. The Case of Terry Sue Berk.

"What was so fascinating about Terry Sue?" Toni asked.

Robby paused. "She was a hermaphrodite." Toni slipped her arm around my waist, like a protective shell. "You knew that, right?" he said.

"Stop using scary words to torment my little sister," she said. I buried my head in ends of her hair. "You're all about shock value, you know that, Robby, and I detest you for it, you lousy piece of shit and you don't know what you are taking about."

"I'm sure my mother can get you copies of the conference papers if you want to read them," he said. His voice seemed so matter-of-fact, not happy or sad, loud or soft, stunned or horrified. "There's a name for what Terry Sue had. Okay. Not hermaphrodite. It's some genetic condition I've never heard of, named after a doctor, an endocrinologist, I think my mother said, named Turner. She was just born that way."

Toni begged off lunch. She told Robby we had already eaten, and she needed to check out a book at the Butler Library.

Outside, the traffic on Fifth Avenue had come to a complete stop. Not even a police car was able to get through. No one was coming toward the museum. It seemed like a strange day, not at all what I expected of New York. People along the sidewalk were hugging, some sobbing. Others had transistors in their ears. A man descending the stairs next to me said, "It's hard to believe he's dead." I had no idea what the man next to me was talking about. I only knew that, for us, things would not return to the way they were.

November 30, 1963

Dear Linda Sue (Toni wrote to me from New York),
I feel I owe you an apology for the outrageous behaviour of my ex-boyfriend Robby Sloan at the Metropolitan Museum of Art a few weeks ago. I know that he frightened you with all of his seemingly scientific jargon about Terry Sue. Believe me when I tell you that he doesn't know anything about genetics or medicine or our family so don't be scared. Terry Sue was not a hermaphrodite. The sad fact is that Terry Sue died from an eating problem that grew progressively worse and killed her. There's nothing more to say and don't let anyone tell you otherwise. There are no skeletons hiding in the Berk family closet.
I hope you will come to visit me next year in New York.
Love,
Toni

P.S. Linda Sue, you should not, I repeat not, say a word about what Robby told us to anyone, especially not to Mama and Papa or Hetty, under any circumstances. They'll just worry or feel guilty and for what?

Fourteen

IT WAS 1968 WHEN I VISITED Toni again in New York, this time to celebrate the completion of her doctoral work at Columbia. I was an undergraduate at Washington University by then, still living with my parents in our house on Tulane. The only thing that had changed was my typewriter. And my perception of Terry Sue. Aside from the one letter I had received from Toni, we never spoke about our conversation with Robby at the Metropolitan Museum of Art. He seemed to have disappeared from her life. The negative feelings I initially had about Terry Sue and her "case" had become submerged in the national mourning for John F. Kennedy, the assassinated president. To think of myself, to dwell on our family's tragedy would have felt un-American in the midst of the outpouring of grief gripping the nation at that time. I doubted that Toni and I would revisit old wounds now.

She had moved from her apartment on Riverside Drive near the university to a smaller place near Fort Tryon Park, alone with her Siamese cat. I appreciated the proximity of her new location to the Cloisters, which suited my dream to become a medievalist. The living room in Toni's apartment overlooked the George Washington Bridge. If I cranked open the casement windows, I could almost reach it. On the narrow window ledge, her cat preened and sunned himself. I worried that he would fall to his death.

On my second morning at her place, I was putting the milk away after breakfast, and in a moment of clumsiness, I spilled a few drops on a box sitting in her refrigerator, a box the same size as a typing paper box.

"Sorry," I said.

"Be careful," she said. "That's my dissertation. I keep it in there in case of a fire." I removed the box and wiped it off. My hands tingled with curiosity. In all these years, she hadn't bothered to explain anything about her academic interests. Her research remained private. It occurred to me, while I held the milk-stained box, that I didn't even know the title of her dissertation.

A few hours later, when Toni went to buy eggs for lunch, I took her dissertation from the fridge. I held it in my hands, trembling, eager to devour every word, every chart and graph, every footnote and appendix. My sister wrote this, I thought, feeling the weight of her scholarship in my palms. My eyes fixed on the top page. "Sexual Identity: The History of an Idea."

In the hallway, I heard footsteps coming toward Toni's apartment and listened to the familiar rhythm of my sister's walk. I wondered if Toni would tell the truth about Terry Sue, refer to her, mention her name. As she turned the key, I craned my neck to see her coming through the door. For a moment, I allowed myself to imagine — nothing more than a tiny fantasy while I watched Toni enter — that Terry Sue was with her.

July 6, 1968

Dear Dr. Berk (I wrote from my desk on 7378 Tulane),
I wanted to be the first person to write you a letter using your new title. So how does it feel to be a doctor, Toni? Okay, you're not a doctor like Jonas Salk, as Papa wished, but to me, you are a kind of pioneer just the same. I mean, a pioneer in

our family, although it goes without saying that Mama and Papa will never understand what you've accomplished. It's a little sad, isn't it?

Of course, I read your dissertation. You must know by now that I'm a big snoop and as soon as you told me that you stored your dissertation in the ice box for safe keeping, it was only a matter of time before I was able to read the whole thing. Which I did when you went to some party with your friends to celebrate your newly minted Ph.D. I said I had a stomach ache that night and couldn't go. Remember? I lied. I wanted to stay home and read "Sexaul Identity: The History of an Idea." (By the way, whatever happened to Robby? Tell me the truth. Did you ever sleep with him or were you just platonic friends all those years?)

For me, the saddest thing I learned from your dissertation was that Terry Sue lived in the wrong century. Had she lived a hundred years ago or even earlier, her condition would not have seemed strange at all. It would have likely gone unnoticed by doctors and Terry Sue would probably have lived an uneventful life. At least that's what I took from your dissertation. I was reading pretty quickly so maybe I misunderstood. It was only in the twentieth century, I think you said, that medical treatments were used to deal with "abnormal" sex anatomy. I can't remember whether you wrote "abnormal" or "non-standard" sex anatomy in your dissertation. Sorry if I've used an incorrect term and offended you. Please don't hate me for it. I do understand what you were getting at, now that I've read your dissertation from cover to cover. You were trying to show that Terry Sue was labelled a misfit because one of her sex chromosomes was missing, right? It was her very bad luck to reach puberty when doctors thought like that.

You probably guessed that for a long time after Terry Sue's death, I was sooo angry at you. I was angry that you didn't *come home for her funeral, and you seemed to disappear when we needed you the most. I forgive you now. I only wish you had written your dissertation sooner so that we might have had a better idea of what was happening to Terry Sue. She lived her life feeling lonely and depressed. Remember how she adored all of those stuffed animals. She never stopped caring about what others thought of her. I'm sure she believed her differences made her a loser. And she didn't really have anyone to turn to when she was growing up, not even us.*

Lots of love,
Linda Sue

P.S. If you ever publish your dissertation, I hope you will reclaim the whole name Mama and Papa gave you in Lodz — Tilya Berkowitz. *I've always liked the sound of those names together, and besides, that's the way you were born.*

Love always,
L.S.

Acknowledgements

I owe a huge debt of gratitude to my family who supported the writing of this novel in a multitude of ways: My brother Les Benick and his wife Judie Benick, my cousins Sondra Baron and Sally Zimmerman and Sally's husband Stan Zimmerman. We, in turn, would not have survived as a family without the devotion of our elders: My parents, Irwin and Dora Benick, my aunt and uncle Hannah and Morris Bierman and my aunt and uncle Fay and Sam Benick. The characters in this novel, their views, personalities and circumstances are fictional and bear no direct relation to any real people.

I would like to thank Phyllis Angel Greenberg and Naomi Alboim for their important role as first readers of this novel, Ken and Marie Sherman for their advice along the way, Marilyn Biderman for her publishing expertise, Luciana Ricciutelli at Inanna Publications for her perceptive reading and editing of my work, Maria Meindl for her gifted and generous encouragement, Dr. Molly Wills for her medical insights, Debbie Gilbert for introducing me to Susan Charney, a Canadian pioneer in education and advocacy for girls with Turner's Syndrome. My enormous appreciation goes to Susan Charney for sharing her knowledge and experience with me. Any inaccuracies in the novel are my own.

I would like to thank Myer Siemiatycki and our sons Matti and Elliot for their encouragement and enduring love.

A version of Chapter 1 was previously published under the title of "Hawkeye," *Jewish Fiction.net* Issue 9 (December 2012).

Gail Benick is an author and professor at Sheridan College. Her fiction has been published in *Jewish Fiction.net* and *Parchment*. Her recent nonfiction publications include articles in *Collected Essays on Learning and Teaching*, the *Journal of Cultural Research in Art Education*, and *Living Legacies*. She lives in Toronto. For more information visit www.gailbenick.com.